DEATH ROW BREAKOUT

AND OTHER STORIES

D0731417

DEATH ROW BREAKOUT

AND OTHER STORIES

EDWARD BUNKER

MYSTERIOUSPRESS.COM

OPEN ROAD

INTEGRATED MEDIA

NEW YORK

All rights reserved, including without limitation the right to reproduce this book or any portion thereof in any form or by any means, whether electronic or mechanical, now known or hereinafter invented, without the express written permission of the publisher.

This is a work of fiction. Names, characters, places, events, and incidents either are the product of the author's imagination or are used fictitiously. Any resemblance to actual persons, living or dead, businesses, companies, events, or locales is entirely coincidental.

Copyright © 2010 by Eddie Bunker's Estate

Cover design by Mumtaz Mustafa

ISBN 978-1-4532-3673-4

This 2013 edition published by MysteriousPress.com/
Open Road Integrated Media, Inc.
345 Hudson Street
New York, NY 10014
www.mysteriouspress.com
www.openroadmedia.com

CONTENTS

INTRODUCTION I

1. LOS ANGELES JUSTICE, 1927 3

2. ENTERING THE "HOUSE OF DRACULA" 51

3. VENGEANCE IS MINE 61

4. DEATH OF A RAT 113

5. DEATH ROW BREAKOUT 120

6. THE LIFE AHEAD 166

INTRODUCTION

Dear Nat,

I'm enclosing a draft of my stories. I wanted each story to stand alone. I could continue and do it all in one large book. I think the best stories are yet to come. How many of your writers have been adjudged 'criminally insane'? It's a funny story, very much like 'Cuckoo's Nest'. As a thief, I was a jack-of-all-trades. I would commit an armed robbery if the money was right and the score was easy – as in the case of one person caught in the parking lot who walked back in to open the safe for me. But I was very careful about armed robbery; it was sooo much tiiimme . . . if you got caught. Especially if you were an ex con. I was a two-time loser. I could play 'short con', the kind of games you see in 'The Sting', which was the best movie about conmen ever made. But short con was a day-to-day hustle, like a job. You'd make a living, but you'd never make a big score.

My day-to-hustle as a thief was 'merchandise burglary.' I'd go through walls and roofs to steal merchandise. Cigarettes and whiskey are best, but I've hauled off outboard motors, shoes, meat (put a sucker in the restaurant business), TVs and stereos, nickel and platinum (from a plating shop), and the contents of a pawn shop. I never burglarized houses. I really liked ripping off drug dealers and pimps, but there are only so many of those.

I usually got one or two scores a week. I had a heroin habit and a good living habit running concurrently.

The weekend started bad. I had a liquor store on Melrose staked out. Next door was an empty store. Me and my crime partner, Jerry, went in there. Most interior walls are lathe and plaster. Chop with a roofing hatchet, rip and tear with a crowbar, hey presto you're through the wall in twenty or thirty minutes.

Alas, we found concrete beneath the plaster. We weren't going to get through with what we had. We packed up and departed, empty handed.

The next night we were back, this time with a 12-pound sledgehammer and a driver's spike. When I started work, after midnight, not only the empty building but the whole neighborhood reverberated each time I swung the sledgehammer. "Ka-boom! Ka-BOOM!" A tiny sliver splintered away. Naw, that wasn't going to work either. Shit!

I needed to make some money. I already owed the connection a couple thousand. My partner had a bar we could enter through the ventilation shaft on the roof. We took the whiskey and other things worth money; we'd moved the back seats of the big Roadmaster Buick and a Cadillac for the haul. We found a floor safe in the office and knocked the dial off. But I couldn't get in. We left. I bought a device that goes down and pinches – and came back to the bar with a fat Mexican named Gordo. I brought out about a grand and some checks. Gordo knocked the pay phone off the wall with the sledgehammer.

The next day, I went to the fence to sell the goods. While I was there, he got a phone-call from a black burglar, who was in an alley behind Western Avenue with a bunch of goods. The fence handed me the phone. The guy on the other end ran it down. It sounded like a taxi job. No harm in driving down to look.

He was on the street, a skinny little guy, whose name I forget. Sure enough, piled in the alley, hidden by a stack of crates, was a pile of loot, including a television, some guns and a silver fox coat. We loaded it into the car and took it back to the fence. He bought everything except the fur coat. I knew I could get more for it from one of the topless dancers out on the Sunset Strip.

The skinny black burglar was a junky, so of course the first thing to do was score. Mexican dope usually being better quality than Black dope, we went to East LA and my connections.

I took him home. We were fixing in the bathroom, me and him, when his old lady said that so and so was at the door. She seemed a mite upset. I thought it was time for me to leave.

As I went out, these two black guys, big and young, eyeball me. As I walk down the sidewalk, I see them come out and follow me. I get in the car. Here they come. I open my knife and hold it on the seat. When the first guy gets to the car, he reaches in the back window and grabs the fur coat. 'My mother's coat,' he says – and I get the picture immediately. My crime partner has ripped off someone he knew.

He opened the passenger door and wanted to reach for the keys. I feinted at him with the knife and he jumped back. I drove away.

A few blocks away, the red cherry lights went on behind me. The chase was on. Alas, I was off my own turf, and no matter how I took corners, I couldn't get two streets ahead. I finally bailed out. They caught me and, of course, beat the shit out of me. About ten of them were hitting me and advising me of my rights simultaneously.

What could I do? I said I was John McCone of the CIA, and I had to get to the trial in Dallas. I had new evidence. It got pretty crazy: when they booked me, I gave my birth date as 1888 and gave my job as Naval Intelligence. I told them they were Catholics and were trying to put a radio in my brain. One guy took out his church card and said he was a Lutheran.

Finally, they broke it off. When they came back, they said, "We talked to your parole officer. He says you're faking." I said that he worked for the church, too.

When they took me for arraignment, I had rolled up my pants, had Bull Durham sacks like medals on my chest and, when the judge came in, I jumped up and started screaming that he was a Bishop, I could tell by his robes. They carried me out, screaming and yelling. I told the DA that I'd been in jail one hundred and eight years.

Proceedings were suspended for a psych-hearing. They appointed two shrinks. They talked to me and said I was an acute, chronic schizophrenic paranoid, legally insane and mentally ill. Off I went to the nuthouse. The rap sheet forever after said I was criminally insane.

In the nuthouse, I agitated all the dingbats into an insurrection. They sent me to prison. The prison knew me. They thought I was a parole violator. The story ends when I bail out of the county jail at night, with the Watts Riots going strong.

Do you want that story?

Then there's the story of how my fingerprints got on a butcher's knife that was pictured on the front page of the Herald Express with the caption: PROWLER'S FINGERPRINTS FOUND. The Hollywood Prowler was a serial rapist and murderer. Whooaaaa!

And I surely want to write a story about prison race war in the memoir.

All best,
Edward Bunker

DEATH ROW BREAKOUT

AND OTHER STORIES

LOS ANGELES JUSTICE, 1927

The year was 1927. In Washington, DC, the Ku Klux Klan put on full-hooded regalia and marched ten abreast down the middle of Pennsylvania Avenue with American flags flying.

In Los Angeles, nineteen-year-old Booker Johnson looked at the front page photo of the march in the *Daily News* and was glad that he was far across the continent in California. Sure, there was prejudice and bigotry there, but there was no Jim-Crow bullshit.

Back in Tennessee, all the colored kids in town went to a two-room schoolhouse, grammar school in one room, middle school in the other. After the ninth grade there was no school. Out here everybody went to school together. True enough, colored kids were a small minority in LA. The great westward migration of The War was still fifteen years away. When Booker reached Los Angeles, he was sixteen years old and could barely read. Because he had to work and help support his mother (his father had died in a farm accident when Booker was twelve), Booker was given a work permit; he had to attend school four hours a week. At seventeen he stopped going altogether. No truant officer ever stopped him. At sixteen he carried a hundred and ninety pounds on a 6'1" frame. His stomach muscles had the ridges of a washboard, hardened from bending over with an 'Aggie', a very short-handled hoe. Indeed, his whole body rippled with muscles conditioned by hard work. From age ten, he'd picked cotton, dragging a long sack between his legs down a turn row, pulling the little balls of white fluff from the bushes and dropping them in the sack. At thirteen he began cutting sugar cane in the hot sun; his sweat attracted insects and the cane leaves had edges that cut the skin. In autumn, he had chopped many cords of firewood that were stacked in the front yard and sold to people passing by.

Now nineteen, he had a job in a Texaco gas station on Wilmington Avenue and 43rd Street. Monday through Wednesday, he pumped gas and checked oil, but on Thursday and Friday he was the on-duty mechanic. Mostly, he changed oil and fixed flat tires, but there were real mechanic's jobs, too. He had a knack for it, and had even managed to resuscitate an eight-year-old Model T the station owner sold him for $25.00. His weekly wages were $32.50, and they were pretty good for a time when the house rent was $30.00 a month. On Saturday, the boss let Booker use the service bay and the tools to work on the Model T. This was a Saturday in September, and the desert heat, which was usually dry, was uncommonly humid. Booker had sweat stinging his eyes. The motionless air weighed him down. None of that bothered him at the moment; he was enthralled by the immense, gleaming engine of the 12-cylinder Packard that had been tuned up.

A shadow fell over him. He looked around. Ned Wilson was in the doorway. A tow-headed young man two years older than Booker; Ned was the weekend manager.

"I don't feel good, Booker."

"What's wrong?"

"Maybe something I ate, maybe the heat. I dunno. I just threw up out there . . . Don't worry, I hosed it down before it started stinking."

Booker said nothing; he had nothing to say and it was his nature to say very little anyway.

"I really wish you could do me a favor and cover for me? Stay here and close up. It's only three hours. I'll give you ten dollars."

Ten dollars! God knew he could use an extra ten dollars. "I wish I could," he said, "but I got a date. Belle don't have no phone."

Ned Wilson smiled, showing discolored teeth, the product of his family's poverty. "I thought of that already. I called Phil. He said you can close an hour early tonight."

Booker felt manipulated. Phil was the owner. Calling him before asking took a lot for granted. Yet ten dollars was ten dollars. He could take Belle to the *Club Alabam*. It was the hottest club on Central Avenue. "Yeah, man, I'll be glad to work for you."

"Hey, I really appreciate that. No shit."

Booker nodded and extended his hand. Ned frowned; then understood and grinned and reached for his billfold. "You takin' all my money," he said as he handed it over.

A car pulled up to the pumps outside. "I'll get that," Ned said, starting out; then he stopped, reached in his pocket and handed Booker the keys. "You're runnin' things now, boy." He gave a mock salute and went out.

At 8:15, Booker started closing up. He emptied the wastebasket, locked the rest rooms and pulled down the garage doors. At precisely 8:30, he locked the pumps and turned off the lights.

The Model T refused to start. When the starter wouldn't turn over, he used the backup hand crank. It had never failed before. He turned it until his arm ached. Nothing. "Damn! Shit!" he cursed and kicked the tire and felt disheartened. What was Belle going to say? How was he going to tell her?

Then his eye fell on the Packard roadster. Sight, idea and decision were all simultaneous. For a moment he almost changed his mind, but he thought of Belle's fine brown frame in the thin summer dress. Nothing could go wrong. The Packard would be back in the garage long before daylight.

The V12 engine kicked over instantly – and roared loud when he pressed the accelerator. What a car. He pushed the clutch and shifted into gear. It was sure easier than the Model T. Outside, he stopped to lock the garage doors. A moment later he turned onto the street, grinning to himself as he anticipated Belle's reaction when she saw the car. She would be waiting on the front porch.

The traffic signals of the era were red and green, without a yellow warning light. A metal flag swung up simultaneously, "Stop" and "Go".

Booker hit the brakes. The Packard stopped. The car behind did not. One second of squealing tires; then the dull crash followed by tinkling glass.

Booker lurched into the steering wheel. His ribs hurt, but that was nothing to the sudden pain in his mind. Oh, God!

He opened the car door and got out. Approaching him in the twilight was a uniformed police officer. Booker's fear was immediate, less from personal experience than from ghetto tales. It was decades before rampant black crime, but not before racist police.

"What the hell kinda stop was that?" the policeman asked. "Let's see your driver's license. Whose car is this?"

Booker produced the driver's license, but ignored the question.

The policeman looked at the license and handed it back. "Ever been in trouble with the law, Booker?"

"No, sir," Booker said. Mama had been strict about having good manners and showing respect. He was apprehensive about police without feeling hostile toward them. LA still had few Negroes and the police, sure of their omnipotence, were often paternalistic instead of repressive. Booker's respectful demeanor softened the officer's initial irritation.

The bumpers were hooked together. The Packard had suffered no damage except a broken taillight, but the police car's radiator had been punctured. Water was running down into the street.

They tried jumping on one bumper and lifting the other to separate the cars. Had it worked, Booker might have gotten away. Alas, the cars remained hooked together. Two-way police radios were not in use yet. "Stay here while I call in," the policeman said. "There's a call box on Figueroa." He set off down the street and Booker watched the figure disappear. It never crossed his mind to leave. His fears were about his boss's reaction. It was embarrassing to have a cop car hit him in the rear, but he had done nothing illegal. It was the cop's fault – and, except for the first few seconds, which were understandable, the cop wasn't hostile, and Booker was sensitive to any current of prejudice in word or tone or attitude. It was a time in history when, despite Jim-Crow and the Klan and good American writers who used "nigger" without a sense of its insult, there was less black crime than white, and it was substantially less violent. Policemen felt no need for bulletproof vests in the ghetto, or to draw their weapons when they pulled over a carload of young colored men. This particular cop felt sorry for most colored guys, and he had no sense that Booker had done anything wrong. His concern was what his superiors would say about the bashed in radiator. The cop reached the call box and made the report.

The Desk Sergeant thought it was funny. He would send someone right away. He started to walk back to the intersection.

Booker smoked a cigarette and waited, worrying over what he would tell the boss about the broken taillight. Would it cost him his job? He'd taken the Packard without permission.

Another police car pulled up. A Sergeant got out. "You the driver?" he asked.

"Yessir."

"Where's the officer?"

"He . . . uhh . . . went to make a telephone call . . . I think."

The Sergeant grunted and went to look at the hooked bumpers. Booker's sense of the Sergeant's hostility was confirmed when the Sergeant turned to him. "Where'd you steal the car, boy?"

"I didn't steal no car, boss man. Honest."

"Where's the registration."

"I dunno. Lemme explain, please. I work in a gas station with a garage. The car was in for the night –"

"The owner said it was okay to take it?"

"Not the owner – my boss."

"Your boss, huh? What's his name?"

"Phil Collins. It's the Collins Texaco station over on Alameda."

"What's the phone number?"

"Nobody's there now. It's closed."

"What's his home number?"

"I dunno. I mean . . . it's back at the station, but I ain' got it on me."

The officer who had gone to the telephone arrived back on the scene. He and the Sergeant, whose name was Bilbo, stood to the side as they discussed matters. Booker caught a word here and there, but the single sentence that sounded clearly was the sentence of doom: "We'd better run him in and check it out," the Sergeant said.

Until that moment, Booker had been worrying how long it would be until he could see Belle. Never had it crossed his mind that he might go to jail. "Hey, man, you ain' gotta do that," he said, his stomach falling.

"No, that's right," the Sergeant said. "We *ain' gotta* . . . but that is what we're doing." As he said it, he came forward and Booker heard the rattling sound of a pair of handcuffs slipping through its notches. A moment later the steel encircled his wrists behind his back. As he rode in the back of the Sergeant's police car, Booker had the ache that goes with tears, although he restrained them. He looked out at the City of Angels, still clean and new, and felt loss and longing, but never did he imagine his future.

After a night in a cell, a pair of detectives unlocked the gate and took him to a windowless room furnished with a table and three chairs.

"Siddown, Booker," one detective said.

"Your boss doesn't back you up," the other detective said.

He looked into their white faces and blue eyes, and the deeply imprinted terrors of the black man in America pulsed through him. He was entangled in white man's justice. All night long he had believed things would be all right this morning.

"Let me talk to him," Booker said.

"It's out of his hands. He doesn't sign the complaint."

"No," said the other detective. "It's the district attorney's office."

"I don't get it."

"You will."

"Take it easy, Phil," said the other detective; then to Booker: "We'll take you to Municipal Court this afternoon. The DA is going to charge you with joyriding. The judge is going to set bail; probably five hundred dollars. You have to put up fifty to the bail bondsman. Can you handle that?"

Booker shook his head.

"Don't you have anybody who will?"

"My mama . . . but she ain' got nuthin'. I give her my check day 'fore yesterday." She had paid the rent with most of it. She wasn't going to understand even a little bit. Still, he had to tell her what was going on. She was probably worried sick.

"Could I make a phone call?" he asked.

"Why, didn't you make one last night?"

"They took my money. I didn't have a nickel for the phone."

"Okay, we'll let you make one on the way out."

But, on the way out, one prisoner was already using the phone and two more were waiting. The detective looked at his watch and said they didn't have time. "They'll let you make a call downtown. C'mon, we gotta roll."

Again Booker felt the steel bracelets. They walked him through the parking lot, his eyes blinking in the glare of LA's noonday sun.

The bullpen of the Municipal Court was like the hold of a fishing boat. Everything scooped from the streets of the city was dumped here to be sorted out. They handed his papers to a uniformed deputy sheriff and took off the handcuffs before locking him in the bullpen. "Take it easy, Booker. Good luck."

"What about the phone call?"

"Tell the deputies. They're running things now."

Booker looked around the bullpen. No windows, walls covered with graffiti. Why would anyone write his name on a jailhouse wall? Did they want friends who came in to see it?

The gate opened again; three more prisoners were dumped in. The large room was already full. The bench that ran around the wall had no space, although a length of it was occupied by a stretched out man in a white shirt splattered with blood. An open newspaper, covering his face, moved perceptibly as he breathed.

Looking around, Booker saw other men with bruised faces and black eyes. Most were scruffy and unshaven. They looked more like bums than his idea of criminals. One younger man was lying on the concrete, repeatedly kicking his legs, as if trying to loosen them, and simultaneously wiping his runny nose with toilet paper. Next to Booker was an older colored man in a stylish jacket. He noticed

Booker watching the man on the floor. "He's kicking a habit," the older man said.

"Kicking a habit?"

"Morphine addict . . . maybe heroin."

"That's why he's kicking his legs?"

"Right."

"It looks terrible."

"It is."

"They don't do anything for him?"

"They might laugh if he asked."

A deputy sheriff and a young man in a business suit stepped up to the gate. The deputy banged a key on the bars. "Listen up in there!" The noise went down, but not completely. "Hey," the deputy yelled, "you turkeys better shut up or I've got something for you."

Silence ensued.

The young man stepped up. He had a yellow legal pad attached to a clipboard. "All of you guys were brought in for arraignment and bail setting. If you have a misdemeanor, don't pay any attention – but if you are being charged with a felony and don't have a private lawyer, line up and give me your name."

Over half the prisoners lined up, Booker among them. Every man had something to say, some story to tell, some question to ask, until the young deputy public defender had to insist, "Just your name. No questions now. Court is going to start any minute."

Despite the admonition, when Booker stepped up, he had to say: "I never got to make a phone call."

"The . . . uhh . . . deputies will . . . uh . . . handle that. What's your name?"

"Booker Johnson."

The young man added it to the list on the yellow pad. A bailiff came up and whispered that court was about to start. "I'll have to see the rest of you later," he said to the several who still waited. Voices grumbled, but the young man departed anyway.

A pair of deputies stepped up. "When we call your name, step out." The gate was opened and a dozen names were called. The prisoners were lined up outside the bullpen and marched through a door at the end of the corridor.

Fifteen minutes later, the first batch returned and another dozen were called. Booker was among these. The deputy unlocked the door at the end of the corridor. "Okay, stay in line and go into the jury box on the right." He opened the door and the motley dozen followed him through. Going from the packed bullpen with its defaced concrete walls and stench of sweat and urine and Lysol to the wide, wood-paneled courtroom with lawyers in trim business suits and hair sleeked back like Valentino and the smell of Bay rum about them was like going from the outhouse to the mansion.

"Okay, move on in . . . move on in," said the deputy as he guided the scruffy dozen men into the empty jury box. All were bedraggled from one or more nights in precinct cells. All needed shaves. Booker and two others were colored. A couple of the others were Mexican. Some of the prisoners had friends or family in the gallery outside the railing. They gestured and signaled and tried to communicate while keeping an eye on the bailiffs, who closed fast on any sign of noise. Booker craned his neck to scan the room, both hoping and afraid to see his mother. She wasn't in the room.

The judge came out from another door, a small man until he mounted the bench and sat beneath the Seal of California between the flags of the United States and California. Then he looked like Pharaoh on a throne.

The arraignments began. The Court Clerk gave the bailiff a list, and the prisoners were brought out of the jury box one at a time in that order. Each one waited at the edge of the jury box while the man before him stood in front of the judge with the young public defender beside him. The deputy district attorney handed the defendant a copy of the complaint and stated for the record that he had been served. The public defender waived a reading of the complaint. The district attorney recommended the amount he thought the bail should be. Sometimes the public defender asked that it be lower, arguing that the defendant was a resident, had a job and family and was no risk for flight. Not once did he prevail. Once the bail was decided, a date was set for preliminary hearing and the prisoner was guided back to the jury box as the next prisoner stepped forward. One man tried to speak, but the judge admonished him to speak through his lawyer. "My lawyer . . . Who's my lawyer?"

"Standing there beside you."

"This guy! I thought he was a public defender."

"I assure you that he's a lawyer."

"Hellfire, he don't even shave yet."

"I'm not going to discuss it with you," the judge finished with a flicking of his fingers and the bailiffs closed around the man. Instead of bringing him back to the jury box, they took him straight through the door back to the bullpen.

Booker was next. He walked with the bailiff until signaled to stop beside the lawyer.

" . . . violation of Section 502 and 503 of the California Vehicle Code, both felonies. Defendant is herewith served with a copy of the complaint." The district attorney handed some papers to the Clerk, who handed them to Booker.

"Waive reading of the complaint," the public defender said.

For bail, the People recommended $500. The judge was looking down at him; the judge's eyes seemed immense behind thick glasses.

"Sir," Booker said, surprising himself. "Can I make a phone call?"

"How long have you been in custody?"

"Since last evening."

"And you haven't made a phone call yet?"

"No, sir."

"Why hasn't this man had a telephone call?" the judge asked, looking at the bailiff.

"I don't know, Your Honor. We assume they had a telephone call when they were arrested."

"Look into it . . . tell the escorting officers to see that he gets his call. He's entitled to that."

"Yes, sir."

"Bail is set at five hundred dollars. How long will the preliminary take?"

"Half a day at most," said the deputy district attorney. "We have three witnesses – the car owner, the gas station owner and the arresting officer."

"We'll set preliminary for 10:00 am on the fourteenth."

The public defender made a note of it. The deputy was already beside Booker, waiting to guide him back to the jury box, and then he took the next man to stand in front of the judge.

When all of the dozen were done, the deputies had them file back through the door to the bullpen. As the gate was being locked, Booker pushed through to the bars. "Say, officer –"

"Yeah?"

"You heard the judge say I get a phone call."

"I heard it. We don't have a phone. You'll get it when you get to the county jail."

"When's that gonna be?"

"When everybody gets done here."

Before Booker could say anything more, the deputy had twisted the key and turned away.

The Hall of Justice at Temple and Broadway was brand new. The jail occupied the 10th to 14th floor. Above that was the roof. The bus disgorged its prisoners at the mouth of a tunnel that ran beneath the building. A big sign with a red arrow pointed to the Coroner's Office, down the tunnel where they walked against the right-hand wall. Across from the morgue was the freight elevator. It carried them to the booking office on the 10th floor. As the booking sergeant counted them in, Booker stopped in front of him and asked for his phone call. "The judge said I could have one."

"I don't know anything about it," the Sergeant said. "Get on in there."

"The judge say . . . "

"Look, nigger, I'm the judge here. Get your black ass in there," the deputy finished with a pugnacious jut of his chin. Zinc oxide ointment covered his nose, and his freckled face was sunburned and peeling. Booker wanted to crush his jaw with one punch, but managed to hold himself back. The satisfaction would not be worth the punishment that would follow. He was already in more trouble than he had ever imagined. He had been so stupid to borrow the car without permission. Why hadn't he thought about it? He'd already been gone for two nights. Morning would be Monday. Maybe his mother knew where he was. That would be terrible, but less terrible than if she didn't know. The jailer's sneering insult rankled him. It wasn't so much being called 'nigger'; back home in Tennessee, white folks (especially the uneducated rednecks) used 'nigger' or 'nigruh' without a sense of insult. It was the jailer's sneer; the contempt and disdain that dared him to react. When the gate opened, Booker glared at the deputy, who felt the stare and looked around. Their eyes locked for a few seconds, then Booker looked away. The deputy laughed to himself, not realizing how close Booker was to losing control. Only a lifetime of family discipline kept him from smashing his fist into the deputy's face. That would wipe the smile away real fast.

It took hours to go through the booking process; the multiple fingerprint cards, the mug photos with the number and "LA County Sheriff's Dept" underneath, the shower and change into jail clothes, the pickup of bedroll (it included cup and spoon), the trek to the hospital where a Medical Technician asked a few questions and had a squeeze down inspection for gonorrhea. After that they were dropped in the tanks. The process took so long because it was done by group. Nobody moved to the next step until the last man finished with the present one.

It was near morning when a jailer opened a lockbox panel and pulled a lever, taking the tank off 'deadlock', and then inserting a key in a narrow gate. "Go down to cell eleven," the deputy said as he unlocked the gate and pulled it open.

Booker stepped through the gate and it slammed behind him. He was looking along the gates and bars of twenty-two cells on the right. Six feet away was a wall of bars running the length of the tank. Between them was a long runway. Booker started walking along the cells. Over each gate was a number – four, five, six. Black faces were visible through the bars. The tanks were segregated. Nine . . . ten . . . eleven. The gate was open. It had two bunks and both were occupied. Booker hesitated.

"Get in down there," yelled the deputy.

"Get in here, 'blood," said the man on the bottom bunk, gesturing for emphasis.

Booker stepped in. The gate rattled. "Watch the gate . . . comin' closed," yelled the deputy at the front. It was a chant always yelled when a gate was closing. The gate was on rollers and slammed shut with a loud crash. Soon enough Booker would hear of the prisoner who killed himself by sticking his head in the gate. Right now he looked around and wondered what to do with the bedroll on his shoulder.

"Put it on the floor," said the man in the bottom bunk. The man in the top bunk was dark-skinned and barely visible in the deep shadows. Light came from a walkway outside the second set of bars.

"Just roll it out," the man continued. "Put your head toward the gate so it ain' 'side the shitter, y'know."

Booker could see the point. If he slept with his head next to the toilet, he might be spattered in the night. He sat down on the mattress; his back against the steel wall. The windows on the outer walkway were open and he could hear the distant sound of cars and the dinging bells of the yellow streetcars passing below. He felt the heartache that precedes tears, but he hardened himself against them. He could not be sure that the other two men, who had now rolled over to face the other wall, had gone back to sleep. He sensed it would be wrong to announce his arrival with tears.

He sat for a while, and then stretched out on the thin mattress, using the County Jail blanket for a pillow. He closed his eyes, doubting he would be able to sleep, but soon enough he fell into it, as much to escape the misery in his heart as to rest.

Late in the afternoon the deputy outside the tank called out: "Johnson, cell eleven, property slip and jumper." It was echoed louder inside the tank by the trusty in the first cell: "JOHNSON, CELL ELEVEN, PROPERTY SLIP AND JUMPER." The Trusty came down the runway to make sure Booker had the news, and when Booker was at the gate, wearing the denim jumper and with the property envelope in hand, the Trusty called to the officer out front: "Johnson, on deck!"

"Comin' open!" yelled the jailer.

The cell gate began to vibrate, and then kicked open.

"Step out, cell eleven."

Booker stepped out; the cell gate shook and slammed behind him. He walked to the front. The deputy opened the tank gate, checked his property slip and said, "Attorney room."

"How do I get there?"

"Follow the yellow line," he pointed to several lines on the floor, red, blue, yellow, green. Each one led through the maze of jail to a different destination: visiting room, infirmary, bathroom, attorney room. All went down the same corridor; then one turned a corner and the others continued. Booker would never have found his way without the painted yellow line. As he passed walls of bars, behind which were other tanks, he saw that the jail was segregated three ways; white, black and Mexican, which was considered a separate race in the southwestern United States.

At the end of the yellow line was a grille gate and the sign: Attorney Room. Beyond the gate was a large room with long tables and benches on both sides and a partition down the length of the table that came chin high to the men seated on the benches. A deputy stood, arms-folded, at the end of each table, making sure nothing was passed across. The noise was the hum of insistent and desperate voices, for here were sweating men in wrinkled blue denim talking to lawyers, bondsmen and probation officers.

A deputy unlocked the gate from inside. "Name?"

"Johnson."

The deputy looked through a batch of forms on his desk. He found the right one. "You want to see Reverend Wilson?"

Reverend Wilson! What was he doing here?

"Do you?"

"See him? Yes. Sure."

"Sign this!" the deputy shoved the form across the desk and

Booker signed. It took him a few seconds of scanning the room before he saw the Reverend's black suit, white hair and chocolate face. "You sit directly across from him. No touching. No passing of anything. If he wants to give you a document, let the deputy examine it. Okay, go on."

Walking down the row, Booker knew something was wrong with his mother. That was his only connection with Reverend Wilson. As he had the thought, he felt suddenly weak and had to hold onto the edge of the table as he sat down. He expected the worst, and when he heard the truth, terrible as it was, he felt relieved. She'd had a heart attack but would be okay.

As Reverend Wilson expanded on the details, Booker's gratitude metamorphosed into fury. Ned from the Texaco Station had gone by Booker's to tell his mother. She called about visiting hours and rode the streetcar downtown. When she got there, the deputies told her that she was too late. Visiting hours were until 3:00, but they stopped letting people in at 2:30. "She told me they were rude to her," Reverend Wilson said. "When she was leaving, she had the chest pains."

"But she gonna be all right, right?"

"The doctors say so. It's in the Lord's hands. You pray for forgiveness for causin' this misery."

Pray for forgiveness! Forgiveness for what? For borrowing the car? No way. He was so angry that Reverend Wilson's words failed to register. He couldn't remember saying goodbye – but when he walked back toward the gate, a different deputy was at the desk – the same one who had sneered at him over the phone call, called him a *nigger* and told him to get his *black ass* moving. Now he had to get up from the desk to unlock the gate so Booker could exit. They came face-to-face and the deputy apparently had no recollection of the earlier moment. That galled Booker even more. The deputy became the focus of all his frustration and pain.

"You wanna call me a nigger now?"

"Huh?"

"Last evenin' in the bookin' office –"

The deputy remembered. His chin rose to a haughty pose – and red flashed through Booker's brain. He hadn't thought beyond saying something, and now he thought not at all. His right fist lashed out. The splat of fist and the crack of broken jaw were loud enough to silence everyone in the Attorney Room and turn every eye in his direction.

They saw the deputy slide down the gate to the floor. Booker was surprised; he had not expected what he had done. There was one moment of satisfaction, followed by a wave of despair, for he knew that this was a terrible crime and he would pay an awful price.

The deputy watching the nearest table came running. Booker threw a straight right hand and the deputy impaled himself on it. His head stopped cold and his feet kept coming. He went down flat on his back, emitting a loud grunt as the floor knocked the air from his lungs. He lay gasping and rolling. The first deputy, groggy and in pain, tried to grab the bars and pull himself to his feet. Booker kicked him in his exposed ribs. He fell back down.

Another deputy approaching him stopped ten feet away. Booker looked him in the eye and saw fear. Booker took a step toward him and the deputy backed up. Booker nearly laughed.

His hilarity was momentary. Two more deputies arrived within seconds. One had corporal's stripes. He motioned the other two to spread out; they would rush him from three sides and gang-tackle him.

Booker didn't wait. He charged first, right at the corporal in the center. He drove head and shoulders into the man's chest and kept going. The corporal was carried backward onto one of the tables. A leg gave way; the table went down, so did the corporal. Bells rang, attorneys and bail bondsmen scattered – and deputies came running from everywhere.

Booker fell on top of the corporal. He pushed up to get leverage and smashed his fist into the corporal's nose. Blood spurted.

A deputy ran up and kicked Booker. He whirled like a cat and grabbed the foot, twisting it so the man fell onto the desk.

Then they were on him, so many that some were unable to reach him in the press of bodies. But lights began flashing in his brain, accompanied by bolts of pain, as the fists and boots and slaps began to land, driven by pack frenzy. Booker lunged backward, carrying one on his back and dragging others. When he slammed into the wall, the deputy on his back grunted and fell off. Someone smashed his eye and sent coruscating lights through his brain. Another rammed a club into his ribs and snatched his wind.

They punched and stomped and dragged him through the jail; on a steel stairway, his head bouncing on each step. Their frenzy was such that they tripped and the whole mass fell tumbling down, one screaming as his ankle snapped. Booker came down on top of the pile. It was outside a tank of white prisoners. They were at the bars, yelling and banging cups and spitting through the bars as Booker was dragged past. By then he was oblivious except for momentary flashes of pain.

Through gates and along corridors, they dragged him to the hole on the 14th floor. They tore off his clothes while still punching, kicking and cursing him. They threw him naked onto the concrete floor and closed the solid steel door. The key turned and he was locked in Stygian blackness. His entire body was a mass of throbbing pain. Each breath sent a bolt of fire through him. A rib was broken. His right ankle was swollen so that both hands wouldn't go around it. The worst pain was in his left eye. It was searing with pain and, when he felt it, the flesh was swollen like half an orange resting on his cheek. When he breathed through his nose, red bolts of hot torment cut through his eye. When he breathed through his mouth, the air over the exposed nerve of broken teeth sent different pain to his brain. Still, the mouth was better when he kept his tongue over the teeth.

Hours passed before he began to focus on where he was and what had happened. He was hurt bad, but even worse was the knowledge that the beating and the hole were simply the down payment. In California he might be safe from lynching, but in 1927 a colored man who broke any white man's jaw, much less a deputy sheriff, was in a serious mess. He remembered being eleven and asking his mother why white men were so cruel to colored people, especially to colored men. The reply surprised him: "They're afraid of colored men. Lord God I wish they weren't . . . 'cause when somebody be 'fraid, that's when they hate and be vicious . . . out of fear. Don't be scarin' people, boy, an' 'specially don' be scarin' white men." She'd told him that in Tennessee, and several times since he'd seen her words confirmed. He'd seen the white man's fear, and the aftermath of that fear, the burned and blistered body tied to the tree. Booker knew the body was Big Luke's, but not because the carcass was recognizable. The white men had feared Big Luke, all 6'4" and 240 pounds of him, and he showed his contempt of them. Even before he had left school, Luke stared at white women, and later began making lewd sounds. As Luke got bigger, he grew bolder – and scared them more. Until they were too scared and came for him at night in white robes. Mama told Booker: "Nigga' was sayin' 'kill me, kill me' his whole life, not in words, maybe, but in how he be actin'. You best take the lesson, boy." Booker later wondered if that was really what she thought, or if the words were meant more to protect her only son from the danger of the rural South in the '20s. Luke's lynching was one reason they moved to Los Angeles, a city without lynchings and with less prejudice, the term used for racism at the time.

For six days Booker remained on the cold concrete in utter darkness. Every hour a jailer banged a big key on the outside of the steel door. He had to call out: "Okay in here, boss. "If he didn't, they would open the door to check on him, and that was cause to stomp him some more. When he had missed the first time, they let it go with a threat; he never again failed to answer.

For three days they opened the steel door before dawn and handed in six slices of soft white bread (the Sheriff's wife owned the bakery that sold the bread to the County Jail) and a cardboard container with a quart of water. Off in the corner was a hole in the floor. It was hard to hit when he relieved himself in the darkness. The stench was awful until he became accustomed to it; by then he smelled it not at all. At first, when he heard scratching sounds, he had no idea what they might be; then something brushed against his foot and he jumped and yelled. It took a minute to realize it was a rat that had entered from the shit-hole in the floor.

On the third day they brought the water but not the bread. At noon they opened the door and handed in a paper plate of macaroni.

Mashed down on top was the ration of white bread, which he used to make sandwiches of the leftover macaroni, wrapping it in toilet paper.

He heard nothing, but hours later when he reached for a sandwich he found it had been attacked by the rats. He ate what was left anyway.

The next morning was back to the bread and water ration.

In total blackness, seconds stretched out. He had no idea if it was noon or midnight. He tried to do pushups, but the bolt of pain was too great as it stretched his cracked rib. The swelling of his eye went down somewhat. Sometimes he prayed, sometimes he sang all the songs to which he knew the words. More than once he wanted to cry out, "My God, my God, why have you forsaken me?"

Through the walls he could hear ringing bells, and the rattle of gates before they slammed shut.

On the seventh day, the door opened. Four deputies told him to come out. As he stood up and took a step, he reeled and nearly went down. He struggled to gather himself; he didn't want them to see any weakness. They threw him a bundle of clothes and, when he was dressed, they handcuffed him and led him through the jail to the court line. As he passed the tanks, sometimes he was recognized. Men crowded to the bars to get a look. The brawl with the deputies was already the stuff of jail legend, and the first chapter in the legend of Booker Johnson. In later years, the story was that he knocked deputies down as fast as they came through the door.

All the tanks were segregated. Then they passed one where Booker had to take a second look. Here the races were all mixed together, but half of those he saw wore homemade makeup and had their shirts tied into blouses in a gross parody of femininity. "I ne'er seen nuttin' like that in Tennessee."

The deputies took him to a floor divided into many cages, each holding prisoners going to a particular courtroom. Instead of putting him in a bullpen with others, they locked him in a small room with a solid steel door.

Late in the morning, they took him to a courtroom for a preliminary hearing. In some jurisdictions, the preliminary hearing served the function of the grand jury, establishing that a crime had been committed, and there was sufficient cause to hold the accused for trial. The prosecutor put on three witnesses. The car owner testified that he owned the car and had never given Booker Johnson permission to drive it. His boss, who would not look at him, next testified that he'd never authorized Booker Johnson to remove the car from the gas station garage. Finally, the police officer told how he had found Booker Johnson with the automobile at the intersection of Washington and Broadway.

The preliminary hearing took less than an hour. The Judge found probable cause to bind the defendant for trial in the Superior Court.

Back in the jail, they moved him from "The Hole" to "Siberia," which was a row of regular cells, the occupants of which were locked up twenty-four hours a day without privileges. Booker stayed in Siberia for the rest of his sojourn in the LA County Jail.

A few days before his next court appearance, he was taken from Siberia to the Attorney Room to see a Deputy Public Defender. Surrounded by three escorts, he attracted looks as he was marched past the tanks. Someone recognized him and the word spread like wildfire. Soon the bars were lined with prisoners cheering and applauding – and the escort deputies seethed.

The public defender had eleven men to see that morning. All he knew of any of them was what he found in the thin folders given him before he left the office. He found Booker's and scanned it for a minute. The case seemed simple and relatively minor. "Did it happen like they testified?" he asked.

Booker nodded.

"Nobody told you it was okay to take the car?"

"No. I mean . . . I didn't think . . . anything . . . would happen. I just . . . uh . . . borrowed it, y'know what I mean?"

"Yeah, I know . . . but you got caught. It isn't the crime of the century. You don't have a record?"

Booker shook his head.

"Never been arrested as a juvenile?"

"No."

"You'll get probation and time served." The public defender believed what he said; it was what he saw from a superficial examination of the facts. He was seeing eleven men that morning, and eight more that afternoon. How could he be anything but superficial? Whatever idealism he'd possessed when graduating from law school had been worn away in two years of representing indigent criminal defendants, nearly all of whom were guilty – a truth he silently accepted after a few months of being a public defender. He had no heart for prosecuting, but he was about ready to go into private practice. If he was going to represent guilty criminals, he might as well do it for those who could pay. Some of his charges he found admirable in many ways. As for the young colored man he was talking to, he saw what had happened and was sure the court would be lenient. He was unaware, however, that Booker had subsequently broken one deputy's jaw and damaged others.

"Here's how it is," the young lawyer said, "if you go to trial, you'll be in jail for another three or four months, even if they find you innocent. That might happen. It's a long-shot, but you didn't really have the *intent* to steal. A jury might be sympathetic. I would expect them to find you guilty – on what you've told me and what the testimony was.

"If you plead guilty to a joyriding, taking a car without the owner's permission, the judge can decide it's a misdemeanor instead of a felony. Joyriding goes both ways. We'll sure argue that, and the DA might not even oppose it.

"You don't have any record. You'll have been in jail for over a month. You've got a job . . . you live with your family –"

"Just my mother –" Booker corrected.

The lawyer nodded that he got it, and then continued with his pitch: "I can't imagine you getting anything but time served and probation. Or sixty days if the judge had a bad night."

Booker was dubious. Without any prior experience and totally unsophisticated about the world, he was sure the rebellion against the deputies would be somewhere in the equation. Yet the young white lawyer seemed to know what he was talking about. He was an educated man. He was a lawyer. So Booker trusted that the words were sincere. Yet he was also part of the white establishment, and Booker didn't trust him enough – not in one twenty-minute meeting – to tell him about the deputy.

Besides, Booker had thought about it in Siberia, especially after the preliminary hearing, and had decided to plead guilty to get it over with. White folks had him T-rolled and there was nothing he could do – but this made it easy and firmed up the decision.

He told the public defender that he would plead guilty in the Superior Court.

The Public Defender made a note in the folder so any lawyer from the public defender's office, who would never know his face, knew the posture of the case. He would waive and stipulate as good as anyone.

So when the Judge asked, "How do you plead?" Booker answered: "Guilty, Your Honor." The public defender patted him on the arm, as if he'd done a wise thing. He was not the same public defender who had visited him – and the public defender who stood beside him at Judgment and Sentence was different from the one at the plea. The Judge turned the pages provided by the probation department, and when he looked over the tops of his glasses at Booker, his face was stern. "I sentence you to the California State Prison for the term prescribed by law, to be remanded into the custody of the Sheriff of Los Angeles County, for his delivery to the Warden of San Quentin . . . "

After that, wherever Booker went in the jail, he met ex-convicts, men who had previously journeyed north to sojourn in the legendary San Quentin. When he told them of his crime and sentence, they were incredulous. "I never heard of that . . . no record . . . no nuthin' . . . first time arrested . . . for *borrowin'* a car –"

"It was a joyridin'. I didn't tell the boss 'forehand."

"Yeah . . . shit . . . but goddamn! The joint right out of the box."

"So how much time will I do?"

"They don't never let anybody out in less'n a year. They say they ne'er woulda got sent to Quentin if the judge wanted 'em to serve less'n a year. You should do fifteen . . . eighteen months at the most. Keep your nose clean."

Keep his nose clean! Sweet Jesus, help me keep my nose clean. It was his last thought before sleep in the ten days he waited after the sentence was passed. His time didn't start until he got there. He wanted to go – despite a gnawing fear of the unknown.

Twelve days after Judgment, Booker Johnson was one of two-dozen prisoners taken from the LA County Jail to the nearby train station, where they were put in a special coach. Its windows were covered with sheet metal, although some had a narrow crack between metal and window frame, so it was possible to peer out at the black night and an occasional farm-light. At one end was a mesh wire cage, within which sat an armed deputy sheriff. The other end had a toilet with a waist high partition.

The prison car was hooked onto a milk-run train that departed at dusk and ran north through sunset into night. In Ventura, while the train made the pssshhhh, whang, pssshhh sound of a waiting train, two more prisoners came aboard, one white, one black. Next was Santa Barbara, San Luis Obispo, body receipts were signed and other men sentenced to San Quentin came aboard. Booker would always clearly remember two things about the trip. One was the cigarette smoke, especially when they boarded in LA. Almost everyone had to light up a Bull Durham or Lucky Strike the moment they sat down. The second thing Booker remembered was the man brought aboard at Salinas. A slight man, who looked even scrawnier with his skinny neck jutting from an oversized shirt collar, he was fish-white and wild-eyed, and from the waist-chains and leg-irons and the three deputies who accompanied him, it was obvious that he was sentenced to die. Booker was across the aisle from him; it was easy to study his face. Booker did so, although he had no idea what he expected to see. Who had the man killed? Booker asked the man beside him, and got in response a vacant look and a shrug. He knew nothing and wanted to know nothing. He was a drunk who had written some bad checks. Because it was his fourth offense, the judge had sent him to prison to get his attention. Now that he was sober, his attention was complete. A couple of times during the night, he sniffled and fought to hide his 'woe is me' tears. If he showed self-pity, he would earn the scorn of his peers.

Booker closed his eyes and listened to the unchanging rhythm of steel wheels on steel tracks, clickety clack, clickety clack, clickety clickety clickety clack. Booker dozed off and slept until the railroad car was separated from the train and loaded on a ferry crossing from Richmond to the San Quentin peninsula. It was dawn.

While the ferry carried the railroad car across the water, the lights came on and the convicts onboard began to stir, which meant that everyone had a cigarette to get the taste of pre-sleep cigarettes from their mouths.

One man pressed an eye to the crack and called out that he could see the east block. Booker had to piss. No telling when he would get another chance. He stood up, the chain between his leg-irons was a foot long, so he took short steps and held onto seat backs. He had yet to learn the secret of walking in leg-irons, which is to stand on tiptoe and take short quick steps, shuffling like a Chinese woman with bound feet.

As he reached the last seat and had to cross the space to the latrine entrance, the ferry hit the dock and sent him lurching toward the gun cage. He crashed hard into the mesh, surprising the deputy, who let out a cry and jumped up, his back against the wall.

"Sorry, boss, sorry," Booker said. "It done threw me, man. I didn' mean nuttin'."

"Okay . . . yeah . . . Watch yourself."

Booker took his piss. Instead of returning to his previous seat, he took an empty space next to a young colored man who, at twenty-five, was returning to San Quentin as a second termer for robbery. Jeff Hawkins, called Hawk, was small-framed, but his muscles were like steel cables. He was dark-skinned, but his features were more Arabic than African: hooked nose, thin lips, sharp cheekbones. Booker had talked to him in the bullpen while waiting for court. "How ya doin', Book?" he asked. "Tell me about it."

"You tell me. You know it."

"Jus' wait a minute and they'll come for us."

It was only seconds. The door beside the gun cage opened. A man in prison guard uniform entered. He had a lieutenant's bars on his shirt collar. Hawk made a sound of distaste. "Whitehead."

"Who's Whitehead?"

"That's him . . . an' he's a dirty –"

Beside Whitehead appeared the sheriff's deputy. Together they counted heads and signed a receipt. The prison guard carried a cane, the bottom six inches of which was tipped with lead. He banged it on the floor. "When I call your name, come forward. Who's Johnson?"

Booker raised his hand. "Right here."

"You stay where you are." He began calling names. As each man hobbled to the door, a prison guard put handcuffs on him – and then the sheriff's deputies removed the leg-irons and dropped them in a pile; property of Los Angeles County. The men now belonged to the State of California. They disappeared through the door. Booker watched Lieutenant Whitehead, a big man with rolls of flesh up his neck from his shirt collar to his cap. God had made him a physical bull, but at forty-one, rotgut Prohibition booze had added eight inches around the waist since he was twenty-two. His lead-tipped cane was draped over his wrist.

When the railroad car was empty, Lieutenant Whitehead beckoned for Booker. As Booker hobbled down the aisle, the lieutenant wore a sneer. Booker expected him to say something, but at the last moment the lieutenant turned and went out. The waiting guard put the handcuffs on him. Instead of removing the leg-irons, the deputy motioned him out.

At the steps, Booker saw why the leg-irons were removed. It was too big a step to the ground. Ahead of him, the other men were being loaded onto two buses. Around them were prison guards and deputy sheriffs. The sun was up, turning the Bay into a lake of molten pewter. Booker wondered why a prison had been built on such a beautiful piece of real estate.

Booker hesitated. How could he get down? Using both handcuffed hands, he grabbed the vertical rail and swung himself down. When he dropped to the ground, it was sloped and sent him sprawling into Lieutenant Whitehead, whose back was to him. Both of them crashed into the ground, Booker on top.

"Get off me, Sambo! Goddamnit!"

Guards arrived instantly, hauling Booker up, then helping the lieutenant to his feet. He brushed himself off, glaring with a red face, his embarrassment doubled by the snickers of the watching convicts. "Smart ass, nigger, are you?"

"It was an accident, cap'n. Swear it!" Booker felt sickly in his stomach. He'd hoped to fade into the multitude of numbered men. In the county jail an ex-con had told him that, among nearly five thousand convicts, it was easy to go unnoticed. With such a minor sentence, he would be gone before the guards got to know his name. That hope was threatened at the outset.

"Swear it!" ranted Lieutenant Whitehead. "I'll be a sonofabitch . . . a convict that *swears* it. I've heard it all now."

The two buses moved along the road toward the prison reservation. San Quentin occupied fifty-three acres behind the walls, and several times that on the reservation. To the left was water, and there were low rolling hills on the other side. To the right was a low-rise building; the prison road ran beside it. The buses rounded a curve and the prison was visible – a long cell-house angling left, and on a ridge on the right were a row of big houses. Their big front windows looked down over the prison walls into San Quentin.

No rain fell at the moment, but the ground was dark and wet, and the rolling clouds, black and gray, announced that rain would fall again. As the bus got close, the vast structure made Booker think of a fortress castle from the Dark Ages. Excitement filled the bus, hiding fear in many. Those who were returning pointed out landmarks, the #1 Guntower in the water, "Got a water cooled fifty caliber machine on a swivel up there." The bus passed through the gate of a storm fence, opened by an old colored man in bright yellow rain slicker. "That's Old Man Charlie," said a voice, "he's been down since ninety-nine . . . for a stagecoach robbery." "Yeah, he could get a parole if he wanted one, but this is home for him." The old wizened face looked up and waved at the newcomers passing by.

The buses stopped outside the East Gate, the pedestrian sallyport in and out of San Quentin. The outer gate was a grid made of steel bands. "Watch your step . . . watch your step," chanted a guard beside the outer gate as the 'fish' prisoners filed through. As always in such circumstances, they were counted as they passed.

Along a tunnel called "Between Gates". Benches are along each wall of the tunnel. At the far end is a solid steel door, but before that, up two steps, is another door. One by one they are called through the side door, on top of which is a sign: "Receiving and Release". As each man enters, a guard removes the handcuffs and points him to three narrow benches. "Close it up and strip naked. Throw everything in there." He points to a canvas laundry hamper. All except Booker. His handcuffs remain on. He is told to stand to the side.

When all the newcomers are seated naked on the benches, Whitehead stepped up. He looked them over, mostly young and white, with faces already battered by life, many with blue, India ink tattoos, reform school stigmata. They hid their fear with haughtiness; they were waiting for someone to mess with them. Booker counted the blacks – eight out of forty-one, or maybe seven. It was hard to tell if one guy was colored or something else. He was brown-skinned and kinky-haired, but his features were sharp, and he spoke English with some kind of accent; it sounded Mexican but was sharper.

Booker came back to Whitehead's indoctrination speech. "This is the California State Prison at San Quentin. It is a *pen-i-tent-iary*. The Court sent you here because you were convicted of a crime . . . or several crimes. We don't give a shit if you did it or if you didn't do it. We care what you do here. You'll get a rulebook, and most of the rules are in there. But I'm going to tell you a couple that aren't in there.

"*Everybody* who comes through that gate wonders if it's possible to escape. Yeah, it happens. Every now and then somebody gets out – but *nobody* . . . *NOBODY* gets out with a hostage. If you have the Warden's daughter and he orders the gate opened, nobody will follow the order. We had a couple guys take a choir hostage. They wanted a car. I told them the only car they'd get was a hearse, 'cause that was the only way they were going anywhere. So don't even THINK you'll get out that way.

"Another thing . . . you may stick a shiv in another convict . . . and if you get caught, you will be punished . . . but we won't take that personal. I won't be mad at you. But IF you even DREAM of assaulting a free person or a guard, I will stomp your brains out on the pavement. If you strike a guard, hang yourself – because your life will be more horrible than your worst nightmares. Kill a convict, that's okay, but if you give a guard any shit, you will wish you hadn't. We'll turn your brain into grits with these." He held up the cane with the ten inches of lead at the tip. He could twirl it as casually as did Chaplin, to deadly effect.

"You may be tough . . . you may be the toughest sonofabitch in the whole world, but you're not tougher than the concrete and steel in this prison. It will wear you out. All of you have an indeterminate sentence. A burglar, you have one year to fifteen years. You can get out in a couple of years . . . or you can serve fifteen years. If you're a robber, you have a one-year to *life* sentence. You can get paroled in two and a half, or you can stay here half a century and watch it get painted twice. You won't wear out the concrete. You can waste your life and get old. You can die here without ever having lived. Most of you are so stupid that you can't read." (Booker listened, and vowed once more to learn to read while imprisoned; he would do that no matter what else happened.)

"You do what you're told and no guard will bother you. If any convict tries to push you around, before you stab him, you come to me and I'll take care of it."

While he spoke, the door opened and two convicts carried in a laundry hamper filled with white overalls fresh from the prison laundry.

"Okay, we're gonna dress you in these overalls. Then you're

gonna go to the mess hall. As you cross the yard, you keep closed up. I don't want you stoppin' to bullshit or play grabass with your buddies."

The two convicts passed out the white overalls to the 'fish'. While they were getting dressed, two more guards arrived and reported to Lieutenant Whitehead. A few words were exchanged; eyes turned toward Booker. The two guards came over. "Let's go."

They took Booker out of Receiving and Release. When the inner steel door opened, Booker stepped inside San Quentin. What he confronted made him stop and look. It was called "The Garden Beautiful", half an acre of brilliant flowers in a formal garden sectioned off by gravel walkways. To the left of the garden was a cell-house from the nineteenthth century. The cells opened onto a long, open balcony; the doors were solid steel with tiny peephole slits. To the right of the Garden Beautiful was a giant mansion of the Victorian era – with a porch running along its front. It housed the Captain and Associate Warden's offices. Convicts circled the Garden Beautiful to reach the Pass Window on "The Porch" of the Captain's Office. The exception was if they were under escort – as was Booker. As he walked between the guards, he devoured his new world – a small city with a skyline. A few convicts lounged on wide stairs to a landing with wide double doors. The sign said, "Garden Chapel". It was the prison church. The convicts eyed him with expressionless curiosity. One nodded acknowledgement. Booker nodded back.

The road sloped and turned between the prison wall and a century-old building that had once been the women's prison. One of the guards unlocked a heavy steel door and turned on a light hanging from a bare wire. Ahead was a narrow passage with rough floor and, on each side, steel doors with eye slits. The light bulb was small and the passage remained shadowed.

One guard led the way; he carried a huge key. Next came Booker. He looked at the eye slits and saw eyes looking back. Behind him came the second guard. Beneath his feet the floor was uneven. It was cobblestone. When the guard inserted the key in a door and opened it, the stench from the shit bucket in the corner rolled forth.

"Ahhh, shit," said the officer with the key, turning his head as he closed the door. "Put him in twenty-one."

They moved to another cell. It had a bucket, but the bucket had a lid and the odor was less. The guard stepped aside for Booker to enter. Instead, Booker stopped. These guards had not been hostile or threatening, so Booker was emboldened to inquire, "What's up? How long am I in here for?"

"Cap'n said to lock you up . . . 'til he can see you Monday morning."

Booker nodded and stepped inside. The cell had a round roof. It was five feet wide and seven feet long. On the floor against the wall were some dirty blankets. In one corner was a small bucket covered with a lid; beside it a roll of toilet paper. In the opposite corner was a gallon can.

The guard, using a handkerchief over his nose and mouth, entered and picked up the gallon can. From somewhere nearby, Booker heard a running faucet. It went off and the guard came back with the can and put it in the corner. "That one's water. The other one is a shit bucket. Don't mix 'em up. Ha, ha, ha . . . " The door clanged, steel on steel, and darkness filled the cell, although a tiny glow came through the eye slit, enough so the darkness wasn't absolute. He listened to the footsteps recede; then the outer door clanged. "Hey, Six Way, who's that come in?" called a voice with a white Southern lilt.

"Dunno, man . . . some colored guy I ain' n'er seen before," answered Six Way. "I think he's a fish, man. He was wearin' one of them jump suits."

"Yeah, it's Saturday. The train come in this mornin'."

"Hey, cell twenty-one!"

"Yeah," Booker answered. He was wary, but he had to reply.

"You just come in, huh?"

"Yeah."

"And they put you in the dungeon right away."

"Yeah."

"That's all you got to say is 'yeah'?"

"That answered everything so far."

"Hey, hey," said another voice. "Lighten up on the guy. He just got here . . . What's your name, man?"

"Johnson . . . Booker Johnson . . . "

"How come they put you in the dungeon."

"They say the cap'n wanna see me 'fore they lemme out."

"Hey, man, who'd you kill? Maybe you supposed to be on the row."

"Shaddup, fool," came a new voice. It had command and authority. "Hey, cell twenty-one. Booker –"

"Yeah," Booker answered.

"You were in Siberia with Smokey Allen. Right?"

"Siberia" was one step above the utter darkness of the county jail hole. It was a row of regular cells, but its occupants had no personal property, no privileges and were locked in the cell twenty-four hours a day. It was cold, too, because they had no blankets and the chill night wind came in through the open windows. "Yeah, I know Smokey Allen. He came on the train a couple weeks ago. Who're you?"

"Sullivan Brewster. They call me Sully."

"Sure, man," said Booker. "Smokey talked about you."

"He talks about everybody."

"Did you fight Dempsey?"

"He told you that, too," Sully said with a chuckle.

"Oh, yeah. We talked a lot. Wasn't nuthin' else to do in Siberia. He's out in the yard, ain't he?"

"No. They transferred him to Folsom yesterday morning."

"Shit!" Booker said; he had counted on Smokey Allen showing him the way around San Quentin. "Hey," Booker asked, "Smokey said you ran the boxing program. How come you're in the hole?"

The question brought a chorus of laughter. Booker wondered what was so funny.

"Tell him, Sully," said one.

"You tell him," Sully replied. "You can hardly hold it."

"I'll tell you why, man. He's doin' fifteen days 'cause he put the flag in the Garden Beautiful at half mast when they fried Sacco and Vanzetti last week."

"Yeah, I had to do that or pay three cartons. That's what I bet. I thought they'd get another stay of execution."

"Bullshit! You just like doin' flamboyant shit like that."

From the rear someone started singing in a terrible voice.

"Radio that shit!" someone else called, simultaneously banging the steel door with his fist.

"Don't you think I sound like Bing Crosby?"

"Ohhh, man, you sound like a fuckin' turkey gobbler."

The words whizzed by Booker. His eyes had adjusted to the darkness, and now he could see that a tiny bit of light came through the eye slit. It was meager, but it spread out, as light does, and he could at least vaguely discern his hand held up in front of his face. It made him feel better for a moment. He'd had enough of total darkness in the county jail.

When his mind turned to the conversations around him, he found they had shifted to matters other than 'fish-colored guy'. He had nothing to do but listen and, within an hour or so, the voices began to take on personality and history. Sully seemed the best liked and most respected, but a man they called "Six Way" was the most feared. Piece by piece, Booker came to understand that Six Way had gutted another convict in the laundry. He was taken out for questioning, and when he came back he told Sully, "They got shit! Ain' nobody snitchin'."

"That sure is some kind of miracle."

"They don't even have a note fingering me."

"Nobody saw nuthin'?"

"Not a goddamn thing. Some fuckin' rat said he saw me over by the shower room gutter."

"That's where they found the shiv?"

"Yeah. But he didn't say he saw me doin' nothin'."

"How the fuck you find that out? You been in the fuckin' hole here for four or five days."

"A week. But my woman got that mouthpiece up here; he went to the Marin County DA's office and got copies of reports. He told me."

"That's where you were. We thought you were out snitchin'."

"Spare me!" said another voice.

"Fuck all you suckers!" said the accused killer, but with a jocularity in the challenge. Then with mock seriousness: "Shit, I wish I could snitch on you suckers. But you ain't got nuthin', you ain't did nuthin', and they're tryin' to stick me with a killin'. They want me more than anything I can give 'em."

"Six Way Jack – always got Six Ways to fuck a sucker around," announced Sully. "I know you're a snake, but I love you anyway."

"Don't do that, Sully," said Six Way. "You know I wouldn't cross you. You my friend."

"I know I am," Sully said. "But I'm still watchful, 'cause snakes have a certain nature. You know about the snake and the turtle, don't you?"

"No. Tell me about it."

"This snake was crossin' California and he come to the Colorado River. He can't swim. So he sees this turtle that he knows. The turtle is swimming around. And the snake calls out, "Hey, turtle, man, it's me, your pal snake. I need to get across the river. Gimme a ride."

"Whaddya think, man, I'm a fool or something. You're a snake. You'll put your fangs in my neck."

"Hey, you and me, we know each other. I give you my word, man. You're my pal. Gimme a ride. I ain't gonna bite you."

"Swear on your mama's grave you won't bite me."

"I swear on my mama's grave."

"Okay, I'm gonna do this."

So the turtle took the snake across the river. When they got to the other side, the snake bit him on the neck. As he was goin' down, the turtle said, "You gave your word. You swore on your mama's grave." And the snake said, "Man, I bit her, too. I'm a snake. I can't be anything else."

Booker smiled in the darkness. It was a good story. It said something. He didn't know exactly what, but it had a message of some kind.

Through the afternoon, Booker listened to the voices. He could identify five, and there seemed to be two or three others who had very little to say. All were white, some had the twang of the South in their voices and Booker, apparently the only colored man in the dungeon, listened for "nigra" or even "nigger", but he didn't hear either. Maybe it was awareness of his presence that stilled their tongues. Or maybe issues of race didn't cross their minds. They sure talked about violence a lot, one story after another about fucking up somebody, or sticking somebody else.

They also talked about sports, especially baseball. Betting on baseball was apparently popular in San Quentin. The New York Yankees, led by The Babe and managed by Miller Huggins, were tearing up the American League.

As he listened, Booker experienced wonder. What was he doing here among thieves and killers? How could life take such swift and unexpected turns? Why had he lost his temper with that white man? It gave him satisfaction, sure enough, but goddamn it wasn't worth the consequences. The papers said "joyriding", but the real reason he was in prison was for hitting the white man. No, not just a white man – a white policeman. Thank God it was California rather than Tennessee. They might have lynched his black ass in Tennessee.

All *that* was behind him. Now he was here. If he kept his hat in his hand and his eyes down on the ground, he could get out in a year or so. He would see his mama. She would never be able to get up to the Bay Area. He would have to watch out for Lieutenant Whitehead. That redneck was bad news for colored folks.

He was thinking of these things when the night he'd had without sleep and the day of tension had their effect and he fell asleep.

During the night he was awakened when the outer door opened with a clanging noise and a cursing drunk was brought in. The splat of fists on flesh, the thud of bodies slamming into walls, the guards' curses and a convict's yells brought Booker – and all the others – to the tiny slots to see what was going on.

Several guards are dragging and kicking a drunken convict to the empty cell across from Booker.

Convicts in other cells are screaming, "Leave him alone! Let him Go!"

A guard rams a lead-tipped cane into the Indian's stomach. When he doubles over, the cane is brought down across his shoulder. It drops him, and the guards fall on him.

A canvas strait jacket appears. They put the Indian in it; then roll him over on his stomach so they can get the laces tightened. He thrashes futilely, squirming around like a landed fish. It makes the guards grin. When they close the door, Booker feels pain and rage.

As the guards go out, a voice says: "You get away with it . . . but some citizen outside is going to pay for this."

Laughing at the threat, the guards walk out.

The next morning, two guards opened his cell and said the Associate Warden wanted to see him. It surprised Booker, for he expected to wait until after the weekend, and to see the Captain, not the Associate Warden. It seemed Associate Warden Douglas was Officer of the Day, and had noted his presence in the dungeon and sent for him. Booker had to shield his eyes from the daylight when they brought him out and marched him to the porch of the big house beside the Garden Beautiful.

He waited on a gravel path, under the eye of a rifleman in an overhead booth, with several other convicts facing disciplinary court for minor offenses: sniffing shoe glue, missing a lockup, failing to stand at the bars for count. One by one, they were motioned through a door marked 'J. Douglas, Associate Warden, Custody'.

Finally, a guard opened the door and motioned him into the office. Behind the desk sat Associate Warden James Douglas, a graying man with the flattened nose and scarred eyebrows of an ex-fighter. He was reading a report.

Three feet in front of the desk a red line was painted on the floor. Booker stopped behind it and waited. Associate Warden Douglas finished the report and closed the folder. It was a thin folder, a file just beginning to accumulate.

"You're not charged with anything, Johnson, but when someone arrives from the hole in the county jail, or another prison, we like to talk to them before turning them loose on the yard."

Booker wondered if he should comment, but could think of nothing to say, so he looked away and kept quiet.

"You slugged some deputies in the county jail," Douglas continued. "Right?"

"Yessir – but . . . "

"But what?"

"I didn't wanna . . . I mean I didn' start it."

"Lieutenant Whitehead says you've got a bad attitude . . . but I'm going to give you the benefit of the doubt and let you out in the general population. I'm also going to give you some advice. You're big and strong and pretty good with your fists, but you're not too tough for San Quentin . . . not unless you don't bleed. Fist fighters don't carry much weight around here. We've got ninety-pound Mexicans with big knives and tennis shoes who'll cut your heart out and feed it to you – if you fuck with 'em. The number one piece of convict philosophy is this – do your own time. You know what that means?"

"Yeah, I think so."

"It means mind your own business and don't be conspicuous. I've got five thousand men inside these walls. If you keep quiet you'll be out of here before the officers learn your name. I don't think anybody's gonna fuck with you unless you fuck with them.

"So I'm going to let you out in the yard. You don't have any enemies, do you?"

"No, sir."

"They'll let you out after Count." He closed the folder and indicated dismissal with his head.

"Yes, sir. Thank you, sir," Booker said and started to turn away.

"One more thing," said Mr Douglas. "The probation report says you read at a third-grade level. We don't have a regular school program, but on weekends some volunteers come in to tutor basic skills. Think about it."

Booker nodded; he wanted to say more but was unable to decide what. He turned away, thinking about the weekend tutors.

When he stepped outside, where one guard waited to escort him, he heard the buzzer summon the next man. As he walked around the periphery of the Garden Beautiful, he looked across the roofline of the prison and thought of a small city. It was that, a tiny city of the damned.

An hour later, two convicts in the barber shop attacked a third with shivs. Blood flew, whistles blew – and the Captain needed room in the dungeon for the two convicts. Instead of waiting until after the Count, the Control Sergeant released Booker in the afternoon. At the Pass Window, he was given a cell assignment and sent to Distribution for clothing. Fifteen minutes later, wearing new denim pants and a chambray shirt with his number stenciled above the pocket, he walked down a road toward the Big Yard gate. The North cell-house was still being constructed, one of the huge fortress cell-houses that replaced the old Spanish cellblocks. One of these still remained; it would be used as "queen's row" for another two decades, and then as administrative lockup, until it, too, was torn down and replaced by the Adjustment Center, a truly Orwellian creation.

As he neared the Big Yard gate, Booker walked into a wall of noise, the collected roar of several thousand voices walled in by the kitchen, mess halls and the East and South cell-houses. The last was the largest cell-house in the world, holding two thousand prisoners. The yard gate was open and he walked in against a tide of convicts pouring out and turning left down a long stairway to the lower yard and the industrial area beyond. They were going back to work. In the distance he could see Mount Tamalpais.

The yard was about the size of two football fields, paved in concrete, and half of it was covered by a high, corrugated weather shed that looked like a huge, open-walled hay barn. At the moment, it still held about half of San Quentin's convicts.

Booker walked straight ahead under the shed. He looked up. On a catwalk overhead was a rifleman. The convict density was less under the shed; it was in the shade and chilly. Most of the men were out in the sun. Along the length of the East cell-house were picnic tables. All but one was used for dominoes, which were slammed hard upon the blanket-covered table. Some of the world's best domino players were here every day, rain or shine, gambling on 'killing big six'. The games were owned by convict entrepreneurs, who took a cut for guaranteeing that the winners got paid. One table was used for chess, on which convicts also gambled.

Booker was conspicuous in the dark, stiff new clothes, which marked him as a 'fish', the name for new arrivals. A few convicts looked him over, but most ignored him as he weaved his way across the Big Yard en route to the South Block, as designated on his cell move pass.

A guard let him through a rotunda – the steel door boomed as it closed – into the South Block. The rotunda also controlled pedestrian traffic to the prison hospital, which could be reached only via the South Cell-house. It was also necessary to go through the rotunda to reach the West Cell-house.

The cell-house office was in the center, under a steel stairway. The office had a dutch door. Inside was a convict clerk at a typewriter.

He was a skinny white man, so old that the tattoos on his arms wrinkled with his flesh. He wore a long-billed denim cap of a cut never seen except in prison.

The clerk got up to take the pass. He filled out a tag and put it in a slot on the wall-board that listed every cell and its occupants. "Eight eight three is on the fourth tier, D section."

"Are you McGurk?"

The wizened old convict looked at Booker for the first time. Only then did Booker see his face. A scar ran down from his forehead through his left eye, which was hazy white with blindness, and down to his chin. Somewhere along the line he'd been slapped in the face with a straight razor. "Yeah, I'm McGurk."

"A guy named Sully said to tell you to give me what I need."

"What do you need?"

"A couple stamps, some toothpaste and cigarettes."

"We don't have tailor made cigarettes. You can get some Bull Durham or Duke's."

"Damn, I don't know how to roll cigarettes."

"You'll learn, or quit smokin'."

A bell rang. From the rotunda a voice yelled, "They're comin' in," followed by the fast moving leaders of the herd; they went to their cells like horses to water. After them came the two thousand convicts, California's worst under age thirty. Most of those over thirty went to Folsom – when they had satisfied the requirement of having stabbed someone. From the sidelines, Booker watched the faces, mostly white – white and Mexican together. Black men were a minority. They stayed together, although he saw a light-skinned brother, with reddish hair and freckles bridging his nose, and his partners were two white queens. That was a term Booker had yet to learn and, when he first saw the trio, for a weird moment he wondered what two women were doing with these animals. When they passed closer, he realized they were men – but only because they couldn't be anything else dressed in convict blues (which they had bleached until they were more blue tint than denim hue) and going upstairs at lockup.

Booker started up the steel stairs. He was behind the trio; two white sissies and a black freak. They seemed very carefree, and Booker knew instinctively that if race relations were murderous in here, this freaky cluster could never exist. The race crazies on both sides would never let it be. Where was cell eight eight three? On the wall at the end of the fourth tier was a sign: 851 to 900. It was right there.

Booker had to go around the trio. The light-skinned brother with the freckles was sucking tongue with one of the queens. Booker sidled past them. He thought he could hear the sound even amidst the cacophony of convicts around him. Someone wanted to bet on tomorrow's baseball game and was being told to get fucked – but the freak and the queen kept kissing like man and woman . . . or something. Convicts passed them without paying attention. Booker did the same. What kind of a world was he in? In the county jail he'd heard the prison myths, but seeing men kiss each other was different than being told. Nobody would bother him. He'd been assured of that – nor did he really need assurance. He knew he could take care of himself. He might get killed, but he would never be pushed around. Or kiss another man on the mouth. Jesus Christ! Ugh . . .

Now he was on the tier, looking at the numbers stenciled over each cell. Eight sixty-five . . . seventy two . . . seventy nine . . . eighty one . . . eighty two . . . People looked him over. A white guy with bad acne winked and nodded.

In front of eighty-three stood a colored man several years older, but forty pounds lighter, than Booker. The knot in Booker's gullet disappeared. He stuck out his hand. "I'm your cell partner, I think. Booker Johnson."

The man nodded and reluctantly extended a hand. "Wilkins," he said. It was then that Booker noticed his cell partner was covered with a brownish lint. It was all over him, including his hair and the stubble of his beard. It was from the jute mill, the prison's biggest industry, where burlap was woven for fertilizer bags and other uses. A chorus of three hundred ancient looms, so he'd heard in the dungeon, seemed to chant all day: "got ya fucked . . . got ya fucked . . . got ya fucked . . . "

Booker didn't know what to say. Wilkins didn't seem to want to talk. Booker looked at the cell through the bars . . . and found it hard to believe what he saw. The cell was about four feet wide. The double bunk was made of US Army cots from the Spanish-American War. The bottom bunk was made up with a cover over a lumpy straw mattress. The upper bunk was bare, flat springs.

The lockup bell rang. All the security bars were raised above the cell gates. In ragged unison, every cell gate was pulled open, the convicts stepped inside and pulled each gate shut. The security bar crashed down.

Booker and Wilkins were locked in. Wilkins stepped into the space between the foot of the bunk and the cell bars. Booker didn't know what to do. He squeezed along the bunk to the rear and started to sit down on the toilet bowl.

"Get up to the bars for count," Wilkins said, motioning for emphasis.

Booker came to the front of the cell. A moment later, two guards came by, five feet apart, each with a hand counter. At the end of the tier they compared their tally and called it down to a Sergeant on the floor. The Sergeant relayed it to the cell-house office. The count was called into Control, the total of the cell-house, and then each tier. Often the total would be right, but one cell-house would be one too many, and another one too few. Someone was in the wrong place.

If the count cleared, the bell rang and the unlock for the evening meal began, tier by tier from the top down. The 5th tier came out, most moving toward the center stairwell, a few climbing over the rail to wait for friends on lower tiers. Wilkins combed his hair and waited for the 4th tier unlock.

Suddenly, McGurk appeared outside the cell. He dropped a mattress on the tier. "Pull it in when the bar goes up." Then, from pockets sewn inside an oversized denim jacket, McGurk produced a carton of green-packaged Lucky Strike cigarettes, a terrycloth hand towel, toothpaste, soap, candy and ground coffee. "I got word from Sully to look after you." McGurk was signaled by someone down the tier who Booker couldn't see. "Gotta go," McGurk said, and was instantly gone.

The 4th tier security bar went up and everyone pushed open their cell gate. Convicts streamed by, glancing in as Booker threw the mattress on the top bunk. There was a hole in it. He stuck his hand in – and came out with straw. "Aww, shit," he said. Straw was a bitch to sleep on. Convicts streamed past him, most young white men whom he thought, back then, were mean looking. They paid him no mind as he pushed the mattress into the cell and closed the gate. The stream of men was all going one way. He joined it and became a human leaf carried along.

Down the steel stairs the voices blended to the clanging feet. On the landing below, convicts awaited the third tier unlock, so they could eat with their friends. On the gun-rail, across a dozen feet of empty space, was the olive-drab uniformed guard with a rifle fastened to a strap that went around his shoulder as a sling. Nobody was going to accidentally drop a 30.06 to the convicts below.

At the bottom, the throng moved straight forward through the South Cell-house rotunda and through two doors into the vast South Mess hall, where two thousand convicts could be fed at the same time – four serving lines and narrow tables the width of the new stainless steel trays, that all faced one way. If convicts sat facing each other across a table, the inevitable result would be violence. Somebody would find someone "eyeballing" him. So he would eyeball back. "So what are you looking at, sucker?" "Fuck your mother!"

Not only did everyone face the same direction, the mess hall was segregated. The sight made Booker pause in the doorway. "Go on, man," someone said behind him. He moved ahead. He got in the line where everyone was colored. As he inched toward the serving counter, Booker noticed that whites, Mexicans, Indians and the occasional Asian, all ate together. Only colored men were segregated. He remembered Jim-Crow from his childhood in Tennessee, where he'd felt no resentment simply because it was the normal way of the world, or so he was led to believe. Now he knew more about its evil and its implications. Goddamn white folks made it easy to hate them.

In a semi-daze, he got his tray of food and followed the man ahead to the long table of all black faces and sat down. Later, when a guard signaled the row to rise, Booker blended in. Back within the cell, the security bar dropped and a convict keyman locked each cell gate. "That's it for the night," said his cell partner as he stretched out on the bunk.

Booker was alone in the dark with his anger. He would die in prison 54 years later, nine of them spent on Death Row for hitting a guard with a bedpan.

He would never get his one phone call.

ENTERING THE "HOUSE OF DRACULA"

They came for me after midnight on the tenth day following the sentence. I heard the rattling chains down the tier, and three deputies appeared. A fourth remained at the front to throw the lever that unlocked the cell gate. When they reached the cell, I was already waiting, my meager possessions in a shoe box tucked under my arm.

It was the darkness before dawn when the two-vehicle caravan exited the rear loading area. It was where the buses, trucks and garbage cans were kept. The stench was gross. I was in the screened off rear of a black and white station wagon. Two uniformed deputies rode in front. They followed the sedan through the predawn streets to the freeway ramp. Traffic was beginning to build, the gigantic Mack trucks and Kenilworth's hitting the northbound highway. They would be in Sacramento by noon. When the sun was a faint orange line in the east, we departed out of Bakersfield to pass between endless green fields of cotton and strawberries filled with Mexican laborers bent to pluck the bolls and berries from the bushes. In the scorching sun, what terrible back breaking labor that was. I would rather be in a prison cell than picking cotton like a *nigger slave*, although that preference did not include the fate to which I was destined. I was lazy, not crazy.

Despite the leg irons cutting into my ankles and the handcuffs pressing dents in my wrists, and the awareness of my destination lurking constantly in my thoughts, the ride was not totally miserable. It had been almost nine months since I'd looked upon the free world. By most standards, it was a dreary length of highway, bordered by small stands selling whatever produce grew nearby, predominantly walnuts, strawberries and melons, but it was better than staring at a cell wall, or dwelling on whatever was in my brain.

When we passed truck stops or tiny communities, a local police or highway patrol cruiser was waiting and escorted us for ten or twenty miles before pulling to the side. The deputies were not related to Lewis Carroll for, though they talked of many things, none were of sailing ships, sealing wax or cabbages and kings. Their idea of a cogent intellectual comment was that all liberals were anti-American. One said it; the other concurred with a strenuous nod.

It was mid-morning when we went through Oakland and crossed the Richmond-San Rafael Bridge and could see the shit-colored masonry of the California State Prison at San Quentin. "There it is, Cameron," said the driver. "Your last home."

"Uh huh . . . the House of Dracula."

We followed the sedan off the freeway to a Stop sign, then went through the underpass to San Quentin road. On the right were old frame houses on a slope overlooking the bay and Richmond's low green hills on the other side. The outlying gate was half a mile from the walls. An old black Lifer stood at the gateway on the signal from a gate-house watched over by a guard in the arsenal gun tower fifteen feet off shore. A female guard who looked like a truck driver and was probably a lesbian came from the gate-house to the sedan and looked at the papers the guards carried. She made a hand signal and the gate swung open. We pulled up outside the East Sallyport where we sat for fifteen minutes until the Watch Lieutenant appeared. Campbell! A miserable sonofabitch if there ever was one. This was the first time he'd been seen anywhere except behind his desk, where it was safe. There were a few inmate clerks in his office, but he'd never been on the yard or alone in a cell-house with the numbered men. And he particularly hated and feared me. Long ago he'd seen in my file that I assaulted a custodian in juvenile hall, a counselor in reform school, a correctional officer in a youth prison. He was Watch Lieutenant; the main man is running things. Above him were decision makers. They didn't have a hands-on job. He had the responsibility for running the disciplinary court. Early on, I'd come before him, charged with messing up a count and cursing the guard. The reality – which doesn't matter in this world – is that my bedsprings had broken, and were jamming me in the back, so I threw my mattress on the floor next to the gate. The cell was four feet wide. Lying lengthwise beside the bunk, how could they miss me? They found me on the third count, when they go cell by cell with a tablet, and cursed me for causing problems. I told the guard I didn't want to hear the orations of Cicero – and he wrote that I called him a motherfucker. So I stood before Campbell so charged. I thought it was humorous, and at worst should cost me thirty days' loss of privileges. But Campbell turned crimson and looked as if he was about to start foaming at the mouth, when he cut me off and said "take him to the hole".

Red fire flashed through my brain. I hunched my back, grabbed the bottom of Campbell's desk and, *oopsie daisy*, over it went, drawers crashing, papers flying. The guards who stand as backup during disciplinary court were instantly administering a choke-hold and dragging me down on my back. I was nineteen and weighed a hundred and fifty.

Campbell wasn't hurt, but he was screaming like a banshee. Of course it went to full committee and, although the Associate Warden did see a little humor in the incident, he had to back the lieutenant and he gave me the maximum twenty-nine days in the hole, and indefinite lockup in administrative segregation, which is different. There, you can have an amenity or two.

I did a year in administrative segregation. Campbell wanted me charged in outside court. Now he was greeting me on my journey to Condemned Row; out here with four deputies and half a dozen correctional officers.

Shit! Double Shit!

He went head-to-head with the deputy in charge of the caravan. The deputy handed him the court orders with the seals and warrants and produced a clipboard with a body receipt for him to sign.

Now he owned me. I was chained and unable to do anything to defend myself except spit on him, which I would do, futile as it would be.

But, *mirabele dictum*, he never once turned his eyes to me. Carrying the papers, he turned back to the sally port, "Okay, bring the asshole in!" With that, he gave the order and disappeared. Everything would now turn like silent machinery.

They hoisted me down because the step was too high for me to manage in leg-irons. I had to tiptoe in tiny steps, rather like a Chinese woman with bound feet. Any other way and the steel anklets would bang against the anklebone at each stride.

Into the doorway they hustled me. Ahead was a gate of steel straps from an earlier time. Beyond was a twenty-foot tunnel with a high, round ceiling and benches bolted along each wall. Near the other end was a solid steel door on each side. One went into the Visiting Room, the other to Receiving and Release. Next to the Receiving and Release door was a urinal and a tiny hand-rinse sink. Everyone walking in and out of San Quentin passed through the

East Sally Port. At that point, I was the only convict inside the tunnel, although every convict who worked outside the walls went in and out through this tunnel.

"Hold it," a guard said, putting his arm in front of me. The Sergeant opened the Receiving and Release door and stuck his head inside. A moment later he pulled back and motioned. "Siddown, Cameron," he said. Then the other escort said, "There's three dress-outs in there. About halfway finished."

So I sat down to wait – and thought of other times. Years ago a black revolutionary, who was also a *cause celebre* among the far left and young Blacks, George Jackson by name, came out here on a visit. He had many visitors, and many rumors swirled around him. He was awaiting trial for allegedly killing a guard. When he was returned to the adjustment center, he produced a gun, chaos ensued and, before it was over, two guards, two convicts and George were dead. The media outcry began, "How'd he get the gun?"

He must have gotten it on the visit, but how had he gotten it into the adjustment center? He was frisked when he came out of the visiting room, and was under a guard's eyes until the escorts arrived to take him back. He sat where I was sitting now, on the bench. It was pretty much accepted, fantastic as it seemed, that the pistol was concealed in his Afro, fashionable at the time.

I don't think so.

Earlier that day, it was said, a black convict who worked in the personnel snack bar passed through and stopped to piss. He took the pistol wrapped in a bandanna, and pushed it up under the sink. He then continued on his business.

When George came out of the visiting room, he was told by an old, white-haired guard, to sit down while escorts were summoned by phone. George sat, then motioned that he had to piss. The old guard was five feet from the enclosed urinal, but he could see George's head and, down below, his legs from the knees to his feet. He couldn't see George's hands or waist. George moved the bandanna and its contents into his waistband.

When the escorts arrived, George was seated on the bench and the old guard told them, "I frisked him already."

So they motioned for him to come along, and walked him the fifty yards across the plaza to the adjustment center.

After all these years nobody has figured out how he got the pistol. I wish I knew the truth.

The R&R door opened and four parolees appeared. All wore khaki pants, sport shirt and windbreaker. Each windbreaker was a different color. I'd been in a cell adjacent to one of them. He looked at me and turned his head away as they passed by. He was afraid to speak to me. I said nothing and watched them step out of the Sally Port into the sunlight of freedom.

I was then out of the other Sally Port door and into San Quentin. Beyond the door was a moderately-good-sized plaza. On one side were the chapels, Catholic and Protestant, and on the other, the Adjustment Center, a newer three story building that held the troublemakers on its bottom two floors – and Condemned Row #2 on the third. A handful of convicts loitered by the fishpond outside the chapels. One or two I knew by sight but not by name.

They walked me down a road past the Quonset hut library across from the education building. One guard walked whilst waving convicts away with a hand signal and the admonishment: "Dead man walking." A second guard followed me and, on a walkway along the North Cell-House, a rifleman looked down upon us. Ahead was the arch of the Big Yard gate, atop of which was yet another rifleman.

The Big Yard was enclosed by three cell-houses and the mess halls and kitchen. The high cell-houses closed out all but a patch of sunlight. Except for a few of the cleanup crew, the Big Yard was empty of convicts.

The entrance to Condemned Row #1 was through the North Cell-House rotunda. An open steel door on the left provided entrance into the cell-house. Another steel door, locked tight, was straight ahead. Beyond that door was an elevator and stairway to Condemned Row. A door next to the elevator was to the overnight condemned cells where those scheduled to die in the morning were moved the night before their execution.

One of the escorts pressed a buzzer to summon the elevator. As we rode it to the top, a bell rang to herald our arrival. At the top, a pair of eyes looked us over through a small observation window. Seconds later, the key turned and the door opened.

Three guards waited inside. Two were young, and one was a true rookie, still wearing khakis instead of the standard olive twill. The third was Sergeant Blair, and his presence surprised me. "Hey, Sarge, what're you doin' up here?"

"Just for a couple days. I work vacation relief. Sorry to see you here, Troy. Never would have thought it."

"Things get away from you, Sarge."

The escort sergeant handed Blair the paperwork and waited while Blair leaned on the shakedown table and signed them. I could look down the walkway in front of the cells. Perhaps a dozen men were out of their cells for exercise. At the far end a blanket was spread on the polished concrete floor for a card table. Four men sat cross-legged and played while two more kibitzed. Near the front was a heavy punching bag, and the only man familiar to me was slamming a gloved fist into it. He was muscular and handsome, with silky, ebony skin. The bag jumped when his fist landed. I think he was borderline retarded, or perhaps just very poorly educated. Out of Compton, someone had taken him to Santa Monica to rob a white kid who was peddling cocaine and marijuana. Richards, for that was his name, almost immediately shot the youth between the eyes. In the jail he looked up to me, and I felt sorry for him.

"All right in there, clear the tier," a guard called out.

"Hey, exercise isn't over."

"You've got one coming in. So grab a hole."

The inmates went into their cells and the guard dropped the security bar, then went inside and key-locked each cell. He could do it without breaking stride. When he was done, he waved and the security bar went back up.

"C'mon, Cameron," said Sergeant Blair.

With the Sergeant beside me, we went through the gate onto the tier. I noticed that, on the other side of the bars and wire beside us, walked the guard with the pistol and tear-gas sap. The guard with the key waited, holding an open cell gate. It was three cells from the bars and gate to the rear. Beyond the gate were ten more cells. Each had an extension jutting out three feet. There was a solid oak door with a tiny window. With the door closed, anyone who screamed was welcome to do so until laryngitis silenced him.

Someone in a silent cell was aware of us out here. The outer door of his cell began to thud, and a muffled voice came through the cracks. "Sarge! Damn, Sarge, lemme talk to you."

"Shit . . . " Blair muttered, simultaneously shaking his head and sticking the big key in the lock.

Clank, the key turned, the bolt shot across, and I was locked very securely in my death-row cage. Twelve-feet long, four-feet wide. On the rear wall was a cast metal fixture – a washbasin with a water faucet that drained internally into the toilet bowl on the bottom. It was prison architecture at its most ingenious. About five-feet high across the rear wall were two metal shelves for personal property.

Along the side wall was the sagging bunk with its blue and white striped mattress. I went to take a piss and saw the layers of crud on tope of the toilet water. I flushed it before I could piss in it. I'd have to scrub it with cleanser and a rag. I pushed the sink button. It worked. The cold water ran out of the drain in the bottom of the sink and seconds later ran down into the water in the toilet.

I hit the switch beneath the twin fluorescent tubes affixed to the wall. The light flickered and sputtered and finally came full on.

Finally, I turned around like a dog and lay down on the bunk. Here I was – home for at least a few years, maybe many. This little cell, that runway out there – and wherever my mind could travel in time and space.

"Hey, next door!" a voice to the right called out. There were only three more cells.

After due deliberation: "Am I next door?"

"Yeah, you just got here. Did you transfer from the adjustment center or come from a county jail?"

"A jail."

"Whereabouts?"

"Bakersfield."

"Yeah . . . yeah . . . you be the dude that iced the two cops. Right?"

From the voice and choice of words I thought he was black, but I would discern, when I saw him, that he was white, no doubt one who had grown up among blacks, as I had done among *chicanos*.

At the moment, however, I resented his easy familiarity. Just because we were in adjacent cells on Death Row didn't imply that we were buddies. He might be a child molester, a short eyes, or a tree jumper rapist, or even a stool pigeon. I didn't talk to everybody just because they were in jail.

"That's what they say I did," was my eventual answer. He felt my aloofness and didn't press the conversation. I began to make up the bunk. I had come to my final resting place. I had entered the House of Dracula. It would be a long, slow death.

VENGEANCE IS MINE

The prison was visible from the highway two miles away, primarily because the long valley was flat farmland with only a cluster of eucalyptus playing windbreak to farm buildings every couple of miles. The prison architecture was not the fortress variety of the nineteenth century, but rather the nondescript post-World War II design. What defined these structures was the tall smoke stack and the gun towers outside the double fences topped with rolled barbed wire.

Every afternoon a wind rose. If it came east from the western mountains it was always cool, because it was drawn from the ocean beyond those mountains. If it came west from the eastern Sierras it was hot and dry, drawn from the vast deserts of the American southwest. The valley, when the fields were green, rippled like a lake under the wind. After the late summer harvest, until full winter hardened the ground, the wind blew endless dust. It kept the convicts off the main recreation yard, shaking the chain-link fences while the rolls of barbed wire on top danced and shivered, waiting for things to settle down.

In 'O' Wing, the segregation unit, a guard walked in front of the cells with a clipboard, stopping at each one. The convicts said "yes" or "no", to the silent question if they wanted to go out to the tiny exercise yard between the two buildings. When the guard was finished, he went back to the front and handed the clipboard to a guard standing outside the barred gate. He worked the switch box that controlled the cell gates. In the lockdown units no two inmates were allowed on the tier at the same time. The guard inside the tier went to the other end, where a third guard let him out. "Okay, send 'em," he called, and the guard at the other end unlocked a control box and threw a lever.

A cell gate opened. Out came a naked young black – the average age of all inmates was twenty-three – carrying his clothes in one hand and his cloth slippers in the other. He managed to swagger, muscles rippling as he walked to the rear gate and put his clothes on the bars. While one guard searched them, the other put the inmate through the ritual dance of a skin search: "Raise your arms, run 'em through your hair, turn around, bend over . . . " When it was done, he was let in and then out a second door to the small recreation yard. He carried his clothes over a painted red line fifteen feet from the door before putting them on. He was almost finished when the door opened and another young, muscular black came out. When not in segregation (the hole) they worked out on the weight pile and the boxing ring. The prison was called "gladiator school", not without reason.

"You ready?" the first black asked.

"Jack ready, homeboy."

The door opened once more; a third black came out, followed by five *chicanos*, one after another. The blacks gravitated to the half basketball court, the *chicanos* to a building wall that served for handball. Usually, they would have started warming up. They had only two hours and they liked to get all the exercise possible. Not this afternoon.

Finally, a white came out. He had stringy black hair that hung down his shoulders, and hair that grew from his shoulders and back. The hair was mixed with a vegetable gallery of blue tattoos, the kind that are handmade in juvenile hall or reform school. Among them were double lightning bolts on his neck and an especially dark and vivid swastika on his chest. Actually, he didn't know Nazi from numbskull; to him, they meant only that he was white in a world where whites were often a minority. He crossed the red line quickly and put on the pants of the jumpsuit and tied the sleeves around his waist.

The door opened and another white came out. He was slender, soft, fair-skinned, and he, too, was defaced by a few tattoos. "Jerry, come over here," said the biggest black; he was the one who had come out first.

The slender white, Jerry, ignored the summons. He went to where the white was pulling on the cloth slippers. Fighting barefoot on the rough asphalt was hard on the feet.

"We gonna have trouble, white boy?"

"That's up to you. But you ain't muscle nuthin'."

The black looked to the other blacks, and they indicated that they were ready. They walked toward the two whites, and the fight was on.

In the gun tower, the guard had noted the tension down below. When it erupted, however, he was not prepared. He was also pouring steaming coffee from a thermos into the cap that was a cup. He tried to screw the cap back on the thermos, forgetting it was full of steaming coffee. The hot liquid spilled over his hands, and he dropped the lid cup on himself.

Still in pain, he looked down. The skinny white and one black were swinging punches, while the other two had the big white boy down and were kicking and stomping him. The gun-tower guard snatched up the carbine. The procedure manual said he should blow the whistle, followed by a warning shot – and after that he could aim at the fighters. Flustered by the burning coffee and the suddenness of the disruption below, he neglected the whistle, although he did fire a warning shot, quickly followed by three more. The sound was a flat, loud crack that sent a concussion through the air, causing a flock of blackbirds to explode from the roof and swoop away.

When the rifle echo died, two blacks were down, and the white was sitting up with blood pouring from his face. A piece of bullet had ricocheted from the pavement and cut his cheek, and the face always bleeds excessively. One black was writhing, the other lay prone, arms spread, while around him was a big pool of thick blood. It was pouring from the femoral artery. The other had broken ribs and scuttled away. With shaking hands the guards picked up the telephone, "Trouble in the 'O' Wing yard. Need stretchers and backup."

The prison was designed with everything in wings jutting out on each side of the long, wide main corridor. Convicts were not supposed to hang out in the corridor, and there were always a couple of guards to keep them moving. When the shooting occurred and the stretchers went past at a run, only a handful of convicts were in the corridor, but others joined them as the procession returned – now carrying the two blacks, one with a blanket pulled up over his face. The burly white, his torso caked with blood, walked between two guards while he held a damp towel pressed against his cheek. It was soaked with blood, some dripping onto the corridor floor. The retinue turned through the door into the hospital wing. A minute later, a convict hospital worker came out and said Toussant was dead from loss of blood.

The prison grapevine is as swift as Western Union. In twenty minutes, every black face was grim, and many fought tears of fury. Toussant had been looked up to by most black convicts. One of the few inmates who failed to get the news in the first quarter hour was Eddie Johnson. He had the afternoon off duty from his job in the kitchen scullery where he scraped garbage from the stainless steel trays before feeding them into the washing machine. He started for the main yard but, when he stepped out into a gust of windblown dust, "Fuck this," he thought, he could miss one day's workout. He had a book by Regis Debray he needed to finish, plus letters to write. He wanted to convince his bourgeois sister that socialism was the best thing for black folks. He would stay in the cell for the afternoon until the main count lockup was finished. He'd come out for the evening meal and socialize in the TV room afterward. A few minutes before the afternoon lockup he heard the cell's lock open. It gave the inmates a chance to go in and out for a couple of minutes – to trade magazines, make a bet on the NCAA Final Four or buy something to keep them high during the night in the cage.

The bell rang and the security bar was raised so the cell gate could be pushed open. Eddie came out, shirtless. He was 6'1", weighed 200 pounds and did fingertip pushups and stomach crunches even when in the hole, which was more than half of the nine years he'd been in prison. He had to stay in shape to be ready for his troubles with pigs, bean bandits and rednecks.

He hurried down the third tier, forty feet above the cell-house floor, to get the Black Panther newspaper from Scott, who lived in the first cell. The tier was filling fast as men came up the stairs. Scott was outside his cell talking to Yogi Bear, whose name and appearance belied his being a borderline psychotic and psychopathic killer, " . . . got him in that fern . . . fern . . . that artery in the leg, man. They let him bleed to death."

"What's up?" asked Eddie. "Who bled to death?"

"You ain' heard, man? Them pigs, man, they kill Toussant."

"Say what?" asked Eddie, his brain reeling. Toussant was his ace partner. "What happened?"

"He was fightin' with this white dude . . . one of dem bikers. They didn't blow no whistle. They just started shootin'. What kinda shit is that, killin' somebody over a fistfight?"

"Toussant?"

"Yeah, Toussant."

Anguish and rage shot through Eddie. It was always the black man they killed. He stood immobile, fighting to breathe. The lockup bell rang and a loudspeaker crackled: "Lockup! Grab a hole! Clear the tiers!" The inmates scrambled for their cells. Eddie walked back to his own open door. He was the last one on the tier. He stepped inside and pulled it shut. The security bar dropped in place. He kept his face hard while listening to the officer's hand counter grow louder, clicking for each body behind a steel door. When the guard's face went past, Eddie smashed his fist into the concrete wall. "*I'm gonna kill one of those lousy motherfuckers*," he either thought or muttered. Either way it was a vow as absolute as any he'd ever made. He looked at his hand. His knuckles were bleeding. He put them to his mouth and sucked off the blood. God, what a fucked up life a strong black man had in America – if he was poor, and the only ones who weren't poor knew how to sing and dance for white folks, or handle the mail. What he needed was revolutionary comrades. You had to control the means of production if a revolution was to be judged successful.

His raging indignation was going to overcome the way he knew the game should be played if the goal was victory, not revenge. He just couldn't let it go. Not Toussant. They'd broken bread together, shared canteen and books. Toussant knew more history, especially about Africa, than anyone Eddie ever met. It had to be deliberate. Toussy had punched one of them a year or so ago. That's why he was in 'O' Wing, and this was their vengeance. "They'll nail me, too," Eddie muttered. "One of these days. But what else can I do except what I'm doing."

There was still enough summer light to leave the main yard open for a half hour after the evening meal. Eddie, big Scott and Dupree, Toussant's nephew, sat side-by-side on the bleachers, their backs to the gun tower. It was supposed to have a device that could hear conversation forty yards away if there was no interference. True or not, they would keep their faces turned away.

"When, man?" Scott wanted to know. The most fired up of the group, he was ready to drink the bitter cup of vengeance.

Eddie held up a hand gesture of restraint. "Be cool. Be patient. We'll come from the darkness without warning, like panthers." he winked and nodded to certify his words. The others liked what he said. They grinned – Scott had bad teeth – and slapped palms in brotherhood and camaraderie.

Prison Shooting Justifiable was read below the fold caption of the *Valley Courier*. Dupree had brought the newspaper to Eddie and waited for a response. The short article said that the Grand Jury had found the shooting of Louis Toussant to be justifiable homicide. "We knew that was coming," said Eddie. "Where's the big man?"

"He was pumping iron in the gym."

"Let's go get him, work this shit out."

As Eddie and Dupree walked the long corridor toward the gym door at the far entrance, many blacks gestured in one way or another. The raised, clenched fist was in vogue. The Black Muslims said, "*Ah salaam aleekem.*" Even though their thing was not his thing, Eddie respected them. They had pride in being black and conducted themselves with the dignity Eddie wished all black men would acquire. They could forget about God and Allah and all that, but he guessed that those things were the price for dignity and good manners.

A guard was at the gym door, collecting privilege cards from each convict wanting to enter. No privilege card, no privileges; including the gym. If anything happened in the gym, as it had before, the prison authorities would know it was someone whose card they had. It cut down on the number of suspects.

The gym was somewhat like a high-school gymnasium – with a hardwood basketball court, although only half was usable unless there was an outside game, which had stopped years earlier when the troubles came to the prison. The other half was a raised boxing ring, mirrors for shadow boxing, punching bags and so forth. Bleachers folded into the walls. There were three handball courts at one end. At the other was a mezzanine, half of it filled with workout machines, the other half with folding chairs and a large television set for sporting events. Everything in the gym was paid for by the Inmate Welfare Fund; profit from the hobby shop and the canteen.

As Eddie and Dupree crossed the gym floor, the klaxon blasted, followed by the announcement: "Cleanup! Cleanup! Gym closes in ten minutes."

Scott worked in the gymnasium equipment room. There were baskets for boxers with handwraps and boxing shoes that they paid for by catalogue order. He passed out towels. He picked up weights and stacked them. His job let him converse with any convict without being noticed. Convicts of all hues came to his window to get their basket or ask for a towel. He saw Eddie and Dupree top the stairs and smiled – until he saw Eddie's face, then his eyes narrowed and the smile disappeared. He knew what it was before it was said: the time had come to strike. As if Eddie read his mind, he nodded portentously. Scott looked at Dupree, who also nodded. "Here's what I think we should do," Eddie said. "After they slop us and make the unlock for evening activities, we hang back in the cell-house and wait. Watch TV; play dominos . . . "

The Inmate Dining Room was thinning as convicts finished eating and straggling out, stacking trays on a cart and tossing forks and spoons in a bucket. Eddie and Dupree came out into the hallway together. Scott was waiting. Eddie made a gesture asking for a cigarette and Scott produced a Bugler package with cigarettes already rolled.

Eddie lit the cigarette and dragged deeply. "Thanks, bro. You dudes ready?"

They both nodded and all three made their way down the hallway to the open cell-house doorway. It was crowded inside with men waiting for the corridor to clear and the cell-house doors to be locked. When that was done, the loudspeaker called out, "First period night unlock. Gym; Education; Choir practice. Reverend Graham's Bible Class is canceled for tonight."

"Look at that," said Dupree.

At the door, two officers were handling the checkout. Actually it was one guard wearing the standard olive twill uniform, while watching what he was doing was another guard. Slight and young, his uniform was khaki, which marked him as a newcomer. He had worked in the prison for five weeks. Anyone could tell that he was intimidated by the convicts. He watched the clipboard and avoided raising his eyes to meet their gaze.

Eddie said, "When the pack is hunting, it can tell which among the herd is weak and easiest to kill."

"I know how they feel when I see that skinny little fucker."

"Me, too," said Dupree.

"Are you ready?" Eddie asked. "You got your mind locked?"

They nodded.

The line going out on night unlocks was getting short. The floor area of the housing units had tables for chess and dominos. The TV room was off to the side. It had small windows with bars that looked like frames. They were designed to muffle the sound from the rest of the unit, but convicts had broken so many that they were finally left unrepaired, and the sound came out.

"C'mon," he said. "Let's go in the TV room."

As they headed for the door it was evident that TV was popular tonight. The room was crowded. The chairs were full and there was standing room at the rear. The TV room was divided racially. When Eddie had just arrived the front center section was reserved for certain whites and *chicanos*. On his second night, he sat in the center section. When someone said, "Say, man, that's reserved." "Right on! Reserved for me!" Eddie stood up; ready to fight. Nobody did anything, not that night – but the next night they were waiting. There was a brawl in the TV room. After that, he had his seat in the front center section.

"What's everybody waitin' for?"

"NCAA Final Four. Duke and Michigan."

His seat was empty but, instead of taking it, he stayed near the door at the rear where he could watch the dayroom. Because of the televised basketball game, there were fewer chess and domino players at the tables, although Lawyer Wilson was there; spread around were his manila envelopes with legal papers and opinions. He refused to appear before the parole board because they had no jurisdiction according to his reading of the law. He would show the legal opinions at every opportunity. The law said he had to appear at the board to be paroled. Except for that, he would have been paroled nearly a decade earlier. The parole board wanted to let him go. He was no threat, no menace, and would cost less on welfare outside.

The trio waited in the TV room until the basketball game was down to three minutes and the Lakers were ahead by eleven and Jerry West hit a jump shot and was going to the foul line. The game was in the refrigerator, or so the announcer said. Eddie motioned and his companions followed him out the door. When the game was over and convicts streamed out, the trio was at a rear domino table, watching and waiting. Their eyes were on the front door. The inmates who had gone to the gym and chapel were streaming back, holding up their identification cards so they could be checked in. Many went up on the tiers, waiting to enter their cells. Others stayed down on the floor. It was still an hour and a half to the night lockup. Finally came what Eddie was waiting for: the senior officer called the switchboard and checked out to the officer snack bar and rest room. He unlocked the corridor door and was gone. Now there was one young guard surrounded by more than a hundred convicts.

"Here's what we do. You –" he was speaking to Dupree, "go tell him that some guy on the top tier is in his cell crying about something. The pig is gonna go see. You'll lead the way –"

Dupree nodded; he would do it, but he felt the butterflies of fear in his guts.

"You," said Eddie to Scott, "get a cup of water. At the top of the stairs there's a little blind spot next to the utilities door. The light bulb in the locked niche – splash some water and it'll pop. You wait back in the shadows. I'll be landing behind the guard. We don't wanna throw rocks in the pond and scare the fish away."

"What?" asked Dupree.

"Never mind," said Eddie; then to Scott, "You come out of the shadows if he goes by you. I hope I get there before that. We're gonna stomp him and throw him over the tier. I heard a fool in San Quentin land on the concrete from the fifth tier. When he hit the bottom, it made a loud splat . . . like some immense egg. This is only three tiers, but they are about the same height. Go make your move. I'll be coming up behind you – I'll bet they showed him my mug shot and pointed me out."

"Oh yeah, Eddie, no doubt they did that."

"I'll be a dirty motherfucker. They can't leave me alone. Goddamn racist mother . . . Ahhh shit, man," he stopped and grinned. "You know what, they treat us better than I'd treat them."

"Let's hear it for that, homes."

He waited. He could see the dayroom and the desk protected by the overhead wire. Scott was going along the right wall, in front of the bottom tier cells, keeping convicts at the tables between himself and the guard. The guard turned just at the right moment, and Scott slipped behind him. He saw him every few seconds as he made the turn to the next tier, taking the stairs in a long stride three at a time. He was illuminated by the overhead light on the top landing. He splashed water upward and there was a little pop and the light went out. Scott stepped back into the shadows and waited.

Dupree approached the desk from the side, spoke to the guard and pointed up. The guard got up, gathered his keys and started toward the stairs. Eddie moved from the rear of the bottom floor toward the stairway at the front. He looked up, saw movement and began to climb on swift tiptoe, keeping far enough behind, and quiet enough, to remain unnoticed. As he made the last turn and looked up, he saw the guard's flashlight beam peering into the alcove where Scott was hidden. The Guard challenged him, "What're you doing up here?" Scott was in the light, looming because of his size, and the guard's voice cracked with fear; he was definitely not in charge.

Eddie crouched and coiled his muscles. At first he had planned to throw his arm around the guard's neck and pull him crashing backwards down a flight of stairs. But if he did that, it would be about thirty feet to the floor. So, as he took the last two fateful strides up the stairway, he lowered his shoulder and crashed into the slight figure in a blind side-tackle. The guard was driven across the landing into the wall, and let out a grunt. "What is this?" he demanded. "What's wrong with you?"

"Shaddup, motherfucker!" said Scott, smashing a fist into the face in front of him. Eddie got up, still with his fingers entwined in the guard's shirt. The guard lunged backward, the force surprising. He tore loose and screamed, "HELP! HELP!" Eddie swung him around and he slammed into a cell door. Inside the cell, Tyree Adams jumped, startled by the sudden noise. He looked through the small window in the door. The guard was down, holding onto the rail with his left hand, holding up his right to fend off the punches and kicks from Eddie and a tall brother he didn't recognize. Dupree appeared from the side, and turned his face for a moment so he and Tyree were looking into each other's eyes from a distance of two feet. Dupree turned away and ran for the stairs, making Eddie curse him for a moment before returning to the kill. While Scott continued raining fists and feet on the guard, Eddie sat down on the tier, back braced by Tyree's door, and used both feet to push the guard under the bottom rail. Surprised, he went halfway under before hooking a forearm around the rail and again screaming for help. In a cell across the way, Walter Semich looked out and saw Scott and Eddie punching, kicking and pushing – and the guard holding on for life. As soon as he saw it, he knew it was the key to a quick parole. He hoped they killed the guard so he could testify against them. Walter was a confidence man, and confidence men see everyone as fools and suckers – especially niggers.

Down below, those in the TV room heard nothing over the sound of the program, but the dayroom convicts playing chess and dominos heard the screams and looked up – but all they could see were vague figures in struggle. There was one last cry as they broke his fingers and he fell, hitting a railing and turning over and over until he hit a bench that broke his back – and the concrete floor that fractured his skull so fluids leaked out.

Seconds later, Eddie and Scott flew out from the bottom of the stairs, both panting and sweating. Convicts were pouring out of the TV room to see what had happened. Dupree, shaking, sidled up to Eddie.

"What the fuck happened? Where the fuck did you go?"

Dupree lowered his gaze in shame. "I dunno. I lost it."

Eddie shook his head and ignored the man beside him. His heart was beating fast. The body was over there, twenty feet away, face turned toward Eddie, with blood seeping from eyes and nose. Convicts were silent, staying away from it, some eyeing Eddie. Scott had moved away to the TV room doorway. Eddie started moving toward the stairs. There would be a call for lockup, and guards with clubs. They might go crazy and beat convicts – but not up the narrow stairs and tiers.

The corridor door opened and the veteran guard with his green twill uniform came in. A minute later, he ran out and locked the door. The convicts laughed – until the goon squad came in with night-sticks.

The Officials threw up curtains around the body so the convicts in the surrounding cells could not see it, as if their gaze would somehow defile it, or perhaps give them ideas that they had power. Killing a convict is a minor affair; killing a guard is sacrilege. None had been killed in the entire prison system for two decades. Flashbulbs popped, men in suits from the District Attorney's office came in. During the night, a trio of guards unlocked the convicts and took them for questioning.

Some came back. According to the Night Movement Sheet they had been out of the cell-house. Others sat all night on benches outside the Captain's office. The Captain's name was Moon. He was small and looked young, and he loathed convicts because he could see a look in their eyes that he recognized but could neither define nor articulate. He was also smart about Civil Service examinations, and was Captain of the Guards before thirty.

Captain Moon would have wagered that Eddie was involved, but was less certain who had helped him murder the young rookie. He would never admit it, but nine years working in prison had instilled racism in him.

Captain Moon didn't lock anyone up during the night. They weren't going anywhere. He was waiting for the "snitch" letters that came in with the mail. Convicts wrote them out and put them in an envelope on the bars to be picked up with the regular outgoing mail. They were sorted in the Mail Room. Seven letters identified Eddie, Scott and Dupree.

"Lock 'em up," said the Captain as he signed the Order. The next day the District Attorney filed a complaint charging them with 187 California Penal Code, Murder, and 4500 California Penal Code, assault with intent to do great bodily harm. Conviction carried a mandatory death sentence with no alternative. The wheels of justice were starting to grind.

On a bright, late Indian summer morning, Sally Goldberg sat in the breakfast nook of her home in the Berkeley Hills, overlooking the East Bay. She spread strawberry preserves on a croissant and poured her espresso. She munched on one, sipped the other and looked at the headlines of the *San Francisco Chronicle*.

The telephone rang in the adjacent room. Sally looked at her watch. It was not yet 8:00 am. She would let the answering service handle it. Instead she heard her husband: "Hello . . . Yeah, Charlie, she's here," her husband appeared in the breakfast nook doorway with his hand over the telephone receiver. "Charlie Connelly," he said, handing her the phone. She licked a bit of jam from her thumb and took the receiver.

"Hi, Charlie. What's up?"

"Did you see the *Chronicle*?"

"I was just starting to when the phone rang."

"Look at the top of page three, the young blacks. They were indicted for murdering that correctional officer down in Anselmo County. Anselmo County gives out the death penalty like the Salvation Army gives out Christmas candy."

"So?"

"One of their mothers called the office. Name of Georgina Johnson. Her son is Eddie. She wants us to take the case."

"Pro bono?"

"Ninety percent. She's got a little money. I don't think we should take it . . . the money, I mean."

"You do think we should take the case?"

"At the very least we should look into it."

"You mean I should look into it."

"I looked at your calendar. All you've got today is an arraignment in the Solano case. Neal has a nine ninety-five hearing in the same court. He can handle both with no sweat."

"Okay. Wait while I get a pencil and paper."

She wrote the information, on a yellow legal tablet. Two hours later she turned off the highway where the sign read: *Anselmo Correctional Institution Next Exit.* Before reaching the prison she passed through the community of neat tract bungalows built by the State for its employees. They were in pristine condition, with lawns like gold greens and flowers in riotous profusion, obviously kept up by the inmate gardeners visible here and there. A STOP sign with a speaker-phone was beneath a gun tower.

The speaker crackled. "State your business."

"I'm an attorney here to see an inmate. I called ahead."

"What's your name?"

"Sally Goldberg."

"One moment."

The static came on. "Park over to the left where it says 'Visitors'. Come back here, and someone will meet you. The Captain wants to see you."

Sally parked as directed. When she came back, a guard with Sergeant's insignia on the collar of his shirt was waiting for her. He had her produce her Bar Membership card and driver's license and had her walk through a combination metal detector and x-ray device. She knew the drill from previous prison interviews and had brought nothing that would make them suspicious. The Sergeant escorted her through the electric gates and up the walk toward the administrative wing and Captain's office. They were in sight of two housing wings and, although Sally was not pretty, her skin having been scarred by acne, which she hid by liberal use of cosmetics, she had a trim body and nice legs. From the cell-house windows came the calls: "Ahh, Mama! Lookin' good, girl!" "Jimmy boy, check out this foxy bitch on the stroll." "I got her, bro'." "Naw, you ain't got her. You *wish* you had her."

The Sergeant led her into the administrative wing. It had the clean sheen more likely found in a hospital than a prison. The Sergeant held open a door marked *Business Manager*, explaining that the Captain's office was in the high security area. "We don't usually allow women in there."

A white inmate was behind a desk in the business manager's waiting room. "Is the captain here?" asked the Sergeant.

"He's waiting for you," then to Sally, "You are –"

"Sally Goldberg."

The inmate opened the inner door. "Miss Goldberg, Cap'n Moon."

Captain Moon motioned her in and told the Sergeant to wait outside. "Sit down," he said to Sally, indicating a chair across from the desk.

Sally sat down.

Captain Moon looked at her. He already knew that she was affiliated with Charles Connelly, a lawyer, probably a commie, who had gotten an acquittal for a Black Panther, for killing a Bay Area policeman. He convinced the simpletons on the jury that it was self-defense.

"So you want to see Eddie Johnson."

"Yes I do."

"I checked his files. You're not his attorney of record, and there's nothing indicating he's requested to see you."

"His mother called our office."

"That doesn't comply with procedure. You have to be his attorney of record, or he has to file a request to see you. I can't understand why you're interested. He is profoundly unlikable – vulgar, a bully and a hater of white people. Now he's murdered a young officer, and I hope we can put him in the gas chamber."

Sally had more to say, but she knew it would be as futile as spitting in the wind; this man wasn't going to let her in.

"I guess I'll have to see a judge and get a court order."

"That's what you'll have to do."

"See you in court, Captain."

"I suppose so . . . but I hope not." Captain Moon touched a buzzer, the door opened and the escort appeared. Sally departed.

Instead of driving back to the Bay Area, Sally spent the night in the downtown *Ramada Inn*. She was waiting in the shade of a pepper tree outside the courthouse when the prison van turned into a narrow alleyway beside the building. Good. It was more than an hour until Court convened at 10:00 am. That would give her plenty of time to confer with her new client. A correctional officer exited the van and rang the doorbell. Several deputy sheriffs came out wearing ten-gallon Stetson hats with American flag shoulder patches. Two more correctional officers stepped away from the van and unlocked the rear. The prisoner's leg-irons were removed so they could step down. One was gangly tall, another dark-skinned and small, while the last was about six feet in height, brown-skinned and handsome. He managed an aura of arrogance despite the handcuffs chained to his waist. Sally sensed that this was Eddie Johnson. With guards pressed around them, they entered and the door closed, the click of the lock loud as it turned.

Sally started to follow and was about to press the bell, but then stopped and lit up a non-filter Camel. There was a knot of tension in her belly and her hand trembled perceptibly. She had to smile, for this display of tension was unusual for her. She had met all kinds of people in all kinds of situations without a nervous reaction.

Sally mashed out the cigarette, thinking that she had to quit, and rang the doorbell. The door had a barred observation window, and this was what opened. The face that appeared was round, with hanging jowls, thinning hair pressed against the skull, and small eyes. "What can I do for you?"

Sally had her bar membership card in hand. "I'd like to see my client."

"Who's that?"

"Eddie Johnson."

"Johnson, huh. Wait here." He closed the window. Sally waited.

When the window opened again, she could see two men. One wore a correctional officer's uniform. "You want to see Johnson?" he asked.

"That I do. I'm his attorney."

"What's your name?"

"Here." She handed over the bar card and the window closed again. When it opened, the correctional officer handed the card back. "He says he doesn't have an attorney."

"His mother retained me. Look, I talked to the judge yesterday afternoon. He said I could see him today."

"He didn't tell anybody about it."

"Lemme see him. He'll straighten this out."

"He isn't here yet. Better catch him when he comes in."

Sally took the card back. She knew better than to argue with such men. They had such minor status and power that when they could inflict a petty tyranny they seldom failed to do so. Moreover, she was an attorney championing a killer of their tribe member, and therefore, their enemy. Sally walked around the courthouse to the other side. Parking spaces were reserved by name or title. County Clerk, Sheriff A. Fernandez, Municipal Court Judge, Patricia Johnson, Judge of the Superior Court, A. Drury. Drury's space was next to a blank door. The Judge would be inside within seconds. She didn't want to miss him, so she waited next to the wall despite being baked in the hot morning sun as the minutes ticked away. Nine am came and went, then 9:15. Court convened at 10:00 am. Damn! She would have so little time.

At 9:30, a dusty Buick pulled in, and Judge Drury got out.

Sally fell in step with him. "Your Honor."

"Yes." He kept walking.

"I saw you yesterday about seeing Johnson."

"I remember. What's the problem?"

"I need your authorization."

"Come on."

He led her through the courtroom. It was empty except for the Court Reporter and a Bailiff in the uniform of a deputy sheriff. The Judge told the Bailiff to take Miss Goldberg to the holding cells and let her see Mr Johnson until the court call.

The Bailiff led her down a narrow, windowless corridor behind the courtrooms. The corridor ended at a gate of bars, beyond which the floor was concrete and the walls were barred cages called bull-pens.

Instead of opening the gate, the Bailiff banged on the bars with a heavy key. From the other end, a deputy stuck out his head and waved. A moment later the deputy and two prison guards appeared with Eddie in handcuffs between them. Sally noticed that he did not affect the ghetto swagger common to most young blacks. He walked as erect as a West Point cadet. The deputy unlocked a cell and entered. A minute later, he motioned the Bailiff to bring Sally.

Eddie had one hand cuffed to the chair across the table.

"Okay," said a prison guard. "No touching and no passing anything across the table. If you have to exchange papers, hold them up so the officer can make sure nothing is hidden within. Got it?"

"I know the drill," Sally said.

"Then have a seat. You break it off when they call for Court."

Sally sat down across from Eddie. The gate was locked and a deputy stood outside where he could watch but not hear what was being said.

"They said my mother sent you," he said.

"Yes, she called us."

"Did you take money from her?"

"No, of course not. I'm here because Huey Newton asked us to look into it."

"I don't know him except from the newspapers. Why would –"

"Because you're on the same side. We're all on the same side. *We* want some serious changes in America."

"I don't remember your name in Huey's case."

"Charley Kelly handled the courtroom work. He's my partner. Here –" she held up a business card scissored between fore and index fingers. The guard at the gate nodded and she handed it over. Eddie looked it over. "Kelly, Romney and Goldberg."

"I'm Goldberg. We've got a couple of other attorneys who are associates but not partners."

"And what do you think . . . that you're going to save my life?"

"We'll do our best. I can't tell what we can do until I know what the prosecution has."

"They've got snitches."

"They've always got snitches. Most of the time juries are dubious of snitches . . . especially jailhouse snitches trying to make a deal.

"You don't have to decide right now. But I think you should let me handle this hearing. It isn't anything, but it will get me on the record and I can get in to see you."

"What about my brothers?"

"I can probably represent them this morning, but we'll have to get them their own lawyers to avoid possible conflicts of interest."

He nodded. "I understand."

From down the range a voice called: "Five minutes."

"You better go," said the guard at the cell gate.

"So I represent you today?" Sally said.

"Sure. Why not?"

Sally got up. "See you in court."

Sally entered as the Clerk was calling out: "All rise. The Superior Court of California, in and for the County of Monterey, is now in session, the Honorable A. Drury, presiding."

The Judge entered in robes and grew tall as he mounted the bench.

"Case number one on the docket, the People of California versus Eddie Johnson, et al. Arraignment for plea."

"Roy Innes for the People."

"Sally Goldberg ready for the defendants."

"Are you representing all three?" asked the Judge.

"For the purposes of this proceeding only there is no conflict of interest."

"Are you two agreeable to this?"

Both nodded.

"Let the record reflect agreement. This is for arraignment and plea and trial setting, the defendants having been indicted by grand jury. Are we ready?"

"Your Honor," said Sally. "I'd like a short continuance to study the case."

"This is only a plea. The defendants are not prejudiced in any way by entering a plea today."

"That's almost true, Your Honor. The only thing is that, if a plea is entered, we will lose the right to file a demurrer."

"A demurrer! On what grounds?"

"I don't know. Perhaps none. But I would like to investigate the possibility of some jurisdictional flow."

"What's the people's feeling in that regard?"

"The State doesn't see any chance for a demurrer being granted."

"Be that as it may," said Judge Drury, "failure to hear such a motion would constitute reversible error, right?"

"Probably so, Your Honor."

To Sally: "How much time do you need?"

"About a week."

The Judge looked to his Clerk, who brought a large ledger to the bench. They looked at it together. "How's the 9th of the month, eight days from now?"

"Very good, Your Honor."

"This matter is continued until next Wednesday, March 9th, at 10:00 am."

Sally wrote it down in her book. As the Bailiff, deputies and prison guards unhooked the three black men from their chains to the table, Sally turned to say goodbye. "I'll see you before next week," she said.

"Can you come back to the bull-pen right now?"

"Sure." She looked to Dupree and smiled. His response was a nod. As she walked out of the empty courtroom, she didn't realize that this was the last time a hearing in this case would have anything but a packed, obstreperous (and sometimes riotous) courtroom.

She went to her car and deposited a quarter in the meter, then headed for the side entrance to the jail area. As she turned the building corner, the prison van was pulling away. "Shit!" she cursed, and her exasperation showed in her body movement.

Inside the van, Eddie looked back and saw her and recognized her reaction. So did the guards beyond the heavy mesh screen.

"Think that commie bitch is gonna save your ass?"

Eddie's shrug was noncommittal, and his face was expressionless. The van left the town for the highway that passed the prison. When it turned onto the prison property, he finally said something. "Officer."

"Yeah, Johnson?"

"Do you know what a fat, stupid pig you are?"

"Yeah . . . At least I'm not a nigger."

"You fuckin' dog!" said Scott. Eddie nudged him with an elbow and shook his head. Scott choked back his curses.

During the rest of the drive the van was silent – but thick with tension. The guards saw the three young black men as vicious killers who had killed one of their brethren. The young black men saw the guards as racist oppressors who might as well have worn Nazi uniforms.

The van went through the sally port below the gun tower. The inner gate slid open and it pulled up to the loading dock. Waiting for them in Receiving and Release were Captain Moon and four guards of the Special Security Squad, better known as the Goon Squad. They wore jumpsuits instead of the regular uniforms, and a belt of tools useful in making searches, consisting of screwdrivers and pliers and mirrors with bent handles to look up and under or around a narrow corner. Now, however, they had on skin-tight leather gloves and carried night-sticks that were officially called "batons".

"It's the trap," Dupree said from the side of his mouth.

"Shaddup," said Captain Moon. He stepped up to Eddie, eyeball to eyeball, except he was shorter and Eddie was in waist chains. "So you gave my officers some shit, did you?"

"If you say so," Eddie could see a look on the Captain's face, a narrowing of the eyes, then the way he hefted the night-stick. He was a second away from ramming the stick into Eddie's stomach.

Eddie struck first, kicking him in the testicles. He let out a groan and jumped back, bent over. The others rushed in, swinging clubs and fists and feet. The black men tried to fight back, but were virtually helpless in the waist chains. The clubs rose and fell and the blood spattered on the walls. Afterward, the guards laughed. They knew that nobody cared what was done to convicts; especially not black convicts who had murdered a correctional officer.

San Francisco and Berkeley combined to make the most liberal and radical community in America. The constituency of San Francisco was the only one in California to vote in favor of pot and against the death penalty. The politics ranged from Yellow Dog Democrats at the conservative edge to straight-out revolutionary guerillas on the other. It was fertile ground for a Defense Committee and a Defense Fund, which Sally's husband seeded with a $500 check. She knew a reporter for the *Chronicle*, and a black organizer of the Students Union; and San Francisco in the late sixties was conducive to the reaction.

Sally also visited Eddie's mother, a strong black woman with younger sons, Charles and William, who she feared might follow their older brother. Most likely it would be William. He was sixteen and read whatever Eddie told him. Eddie could write, he could convince her but, right or wrong, he was going to be destroyed. "No, they won't let him get away," said his mother with anguish in her voice. She brought out a packet of letters Eddie had written and, after Sally had read a paragraph or two, she said, "Let me take these. I'll get them back to you. I think they will get us sympathetic attention, and money for the defense."

"If they'll help, take 'em."

Sally read many of them in the hotel room and during the short flight to San Francisco. Before Sally entered her front door, Eddie's letters were represented by a good literary agent, who would come up with the idea of asking William Styron to write an introduction, which proved a great idea and inclined reviewers and critics to take the work seriously. It needed editing, but so does the work of many acclaimed authors. Despite some spelling and grammatical errors, the letters were a powerful exploration of a strong-willed young black man trying to formulate a view of the world that fit the realities of his existence. Sally was sure that the letters would arouse a tide of sympathy.

As the prison van pulled into the plaza outside the civic center buildings, the brothers in the van looked out at the two-dozen sign-carrying protesters and the television news crew. The television reporter was talking to Sally Goldberg.

"Ahhh, man . . . check it out!" said Big Scott. "We got some help."

"Yeah . . . but they all be white," said Dupree.

"So what? The shitstorm we're in, I'll take anybody's help."

A news photographer was waiting as they exited the van at the side loading dock. "Hey!" he called; they all turned and he took a picture of their battered faces. It would be on the front page of the *San Francisco Chronicle* the following morning. The guards were indifferent when the picture was taken. Beating on convicts was routine. The public had no sympathy for the convicts, and the courts invariably took the position that prisons were better left to the experts – prison officials.

That wasn't Sally's reaction when she saw Eddie through the bullpen bars. "Oh my God, what happened to you?" His right eye was shut beneath a swelling the size of a golf ball.

"They said shut up and I thought they said stand up."

"Tee hee, haw haw – but it ain't funny, McGee. Tell me what the hell happened."

So he told her in detail. "Do you mean to say," she inserted, "that they did this to you while you were cuffed up?"

"There were too many for us to win, but you better believe there would have been some marks on their lily white –"

"Maybe we can twist it to our advantage," she said, and in the courtroom she was both flamboyant and fiery: "Imagine, your Honor, how it looks to the world to have black men chained like slaves in a courtroom in the last half of the twentieth century. Look at their faces. They could very easily have died, and the Court would have had a modern lynching –"

"Miss . . . Miss Goldberg. Lynch is a pretty extreme term."

"What word better describes it? Let the record reflect that their faces look like hamburgers."

"No, the record should not reflect that. They have some bruises, that is all. I'm informed that they assaulted the correctional officers who transported them, and they were subdued with a minimum amount of necessary force."

"Your Honor," called the young Deputy District Attorney, "if it please the Court, this morning's hearing is for pleas and setting trial dates – and deciding what Mr Johnson's co-defendants are going to do about representation. We can set a date for hearing counsel's claims about collateral matters."

"That's true," said Judge Drury. "We can stipulate there is no presumption of waiver of any right otherwise available."

"So stipulated," chirped the prosecutor.

"I'll stipulate to that – as far as it goes. But I want the Court to order a complete medical examination independent of the prison, plus a photographic record of their injuries, and those of the officers, if any, as of today."

"There's no need for that," said the deputy district attorney.

"I believe it is more than merited. I think it's worthy of investigation by the civil rights division of the Department of Justice, which I'm going to file for when I get back to San Francisco."

Judge Drury put his head back and looked down his nose at her. "I'll see you both in chambers in fifteen minutes, after bladder relief. Defendants need not be present."

As Sally turned to go, Eddie gestured the question, *what's up?* All Sally could do was shrug her own confusion. In the courthouse corridor she asked the deputy district attorney, "What's on his mind?"

"I have no idea. He definitely marches to his own drummer."

The judge was out of his robes and putting on his suit jacket when they entered his chambers. "Look," he said, "I can see that this is going to be a circus . . . and I don't want a circus in my courtroom or my courthouse," he looked at the young deputy district attorney and shook his head while clucking sadly. "Do you?"

"We're not going to be intimidated by troublemakers and noisy protesters. If our local police can't handle it, we can call in reinforcements from the highway patrol, or whatever."

"That's true enough, but I don't like it . . . so I am going to order a change of venue to San Francisco. You'll still prosecute."

"I think that's a wise decision," Sally said. Her heart was beating in exultation. Even San Francisco was a long shot, but it gave her hope.

Eddie, however, was still pessimistic. "It don't matter where the trial, they're going to give me the gas chamber."

Every man in the Adjustment Center was entitled to an hour of exercise each day. Actually, they got an hour every other day. When the Day Watch came on duty, they opened one cell gate. The prisoner came out onto the tier for an hour. He could shower – the first cell had been converted into a shower – and stay out on the tier until the hour ended. He could pace up and down or stop outside someone's cell and talk through the bars. When the hour ended, he was locked in his cell, and the next man came out. As there were seventeen men and only eight hours on the Watch, it took two days to exercise everyone.

A black convict named James Brown was out on the tier. He was still drying his hair when he stopped outside Eddie's cell. "Look here," he said, motioning Eddie to come close to the bars where they whispered. Brown leaned close. "Look here, my woman will bring us a pistol. Can we do anything with it?"

Eddie snorted. "Can we even get it?"

"I dunno. That's why I'm tellin' you, you know what I mean?"

"Yeah . . . well . . . shit . . . I don't know. Lemme think on it."

"If we goin to die, let's take some white mothafucka's with us."

In the night, while the men talked from cage to cage, usually about violence, Eddie thought about getting the pistol. His first thought was the difficulty of getting it into San Quentin. Then he realized it seemed difficult because it had never been done. The idea of a firearm inside prison walls drove the officials up the wall. Still, abundant drugs got in. Why not get a pistol in the same way? Of course, most drug packages were small and light, but not so the kilo of marijuana smuggled in through a brother from Oakland. Someone on the outside had driven to the edge of the prison reservation, to the "village" with houses for personnel, or the firing range, or the marsh beside the reservation. The car turned off the highway, its headlights were doused and it bounced along the rutted dirt-road past the sign: "NO TRESPASSING. California Dept. of Corrections". The package was dropped off at a designated spot, probably a trash can. When the prison trash truck made its rounds, it was easy for the convict worker to pick it up without the guard seeing anything. The trucks were not searched coming in the back gate. If a brother worked the truck it would be easy to do. No black would refuse Eddie, not unless he was ready to die or seek protection from the Captain. The latter choice would mean death. If a white boy refused or sought protection, they would likely kill him. Most whites hated Eddie as much, or more, than the prison guards, since his case was making headlines all over the world.

Yes, he could probably get it inside the walls, but getting it into the Adjustment Center, that was something else entirely. It was as secure as Death Row. Indeed, the third floor was Death Row. Everything that came in was searched by hand and with a metal detector. No doubt there was some way to smuggle it into the building, but he had never thought about it. But then – so what? He could cause confusion and take out a couple of guards, maybe, but he wouldn't end up anywhere except back in his cell or in the morgue. He knew that. Still . . . what were his choices? Better to die with a gun in your hand, than being strapped into the gas chamber and have a lot of white faces staring at you as you died. If he was to go, it would be as the black leader he was to his people.

***

On many nights the fog came from the sea and rolled across the Bay. The outside prison lights grew dim as the fog thickened around them. Soon the only sounds were the water slapping against the pilings and hulls, and the foghorn lament. San Quentin's reservation covered a couple of thousand acres. The security area, inside the walls, was a fraction of the total. The rest was a housing development for personnel and big Victorian houses for the Wardens and Captain. They sat on a hillside and looked down inside the walls. There was a farm, and even some wetlands. All of it was hidden by heavy fog. Inside the walls there was special "fog-line" security. Certain gates were locked, others were out of bounds, and extra guards were posted in spots made blind by the fog.

The extra security was in the prison interior, not the outside reservation. A rental car with changed license plates turned off the little-used public road onto the prison property, "No Trespassing, California Dept. of Corrections" read the bullet-pocked sign. The car parked off to the side where, in the fog, it would not be noticed by the occasional correctional officer coming home. A figure got out carrying a small Macy's bag. The figure hurried along the narrow, rutted roadway. Headlights appeared like a pair of bouncing yellow eyes. The figure ducked to the side and lay prone until the vehicle passed by.

The terrain here was a combination of mud flat and wetland. The figure followed the road bed around a jutting headland and vaguely perceived a mercury vapor street light over the entrance. Its reach was very small in the fog. The figure circled outside of the glow and stayed in the gray of the fog and the black of night as he covered the last quarter mile and put the package where it was supposed to go.

In the morning, the prison trucks went out of the rear sally portgate to perform their duties. One was the trash truck; it picked up barrels of trash, dumped the contents into the crusher and, eventually, made it to a trash dump in Richmond, then returned to San Quentin. The laundry truck came out, made it to the officers' reservation, delivering clean laundry and picking up dirty. It even stopped at the Warden and Associate Warden's houses to get dirty underwear and bedding. Other trucks took out work crews cleaning up drainage ditches clogged with weeds, or shoveled hot asphalt into potholes.

A convict on one of these trucks picked up the package and carried it back through the sally port-gate and into the walls of San Quentin State Prison. A gun inside the walls was the rarest contraband of all. It was a hundred times more likely that convicts would smuggle in heroin than a gun. The last pistol smuggled in was turned in as a ploy to get parole. It worked. This pistol was no ploy. It was the key to a breakout plan of such desperate bravado that it could not conceivably work.

In his cell on the bottom floor of the Adjustment Center, Eddie was doing a hundred fingertip push-ups, twenty at a set. It was morning and nearly everyone else was asleep. They talked all night and slept until the afternoon. Nobody cared.

He was unable to see out into the plaza and Garden Beautiful because of the eight-foot redwood fence outside the building, but the windows were open and he could hear convicts crossing the walkways of the formal garden toward the pedestrian sally port. They worked outside the walls in the Employee's Snack Bar, Gas Station, Barber Shop, or as House Boy for the very top officials.

He stopped his push-ups and stood listening at the cell bars. Every morning a few black convicts called out, "Stay strong, Eddie!" or "Power to the People, Eddie." These, however, were not the words he wanted to hear. The tension of anticipation was a great vice crushing his chest. Where the fuck *was* he . . . ?

He heard the key turn in the grille gate at the front. It was done softly – but a pig was on the tier.

"Hey, Eddie," yelled the voice he waited for. "Where ya be, comrade?"

He stayed silent. He hoped the man outside would do the same. No such luck. "Hey, Eddie, are you there?"

Fuck it. "Yeah, me and this pig."

"I'm gone," he whispered, "but Killer Shorty say it be okay. He has the package and he's ready to deliver when you want it."

"Be careful. Be silent."

"Quiet as the grave."

Simultaneously, he heard the jangling keys on a chain and the guard came into view. It was Sylvester, Esque's only black officer.

"Eddie, chill on that yelling or I'll have to shut the tier down."

He nodded. "Yeah, okay. I'm just keepin' up morale."

"You start trial in a couple weeks, don't you?"

"Uh huh . . . in white man's court . . . "

"You never know what a jury will do. After all, the trial is in San Francisco . . . very liberal."

"We both know that the verdict will be guilty. Say, how come a brother like you works in a prison?"

"I've got a family, and it's a civil service job with benefits."

"So you don't mind helpin' whitey keep his boot on the black man's neck."

"I don't see it that way. Most of the brothers are in here for preying on black folks . . . including you."

"What're you talking about?"

"I looked in your file. Correct me if I'm wrong, but didn't you rob a black man's liquor store?"

"Yeah, I did. I was nineteen years old and I didn't know any better. I wouldn't do it now – and I damn sure wouldn't sit and watch black men in a cage."

"I'd rather watch than be watched . . . and my kids won't ever be on welfare."

"That's good. I give that to you even if the Man has you brainwashed with his bullshit."

"Thanks, Eddie, even if Chairman Mao has *you* brainwashed into that communist bullshit."

Sylvester tapped his key on the cell bars as a goodbye and went about his routine patrol.

Nobody on the tier knew about the pistol. He'd withheld the information for more than one reason. He was certain that none of them would tell *the Man*, but it was possible that one or more might confide to someone he trusted absolutely, and that someone might confide to someone else, and someone might want a parole more than a good name among his comrades. He'd been stung more than once by trusting some piece of garbage that he thought was solid. He hoped there was no betrayal this time, and he was trying to make sure there wouldn't be. Still, the fuse was already ignited and he would have to be very careful before things exploded. The plan was fantastic, but John Dillinger had escaped with a soap gun blackened with shoe polish.

He kneeled in the narrow space next to the bunk and extended his arms for another set of fingertip push-ups. This time he increased the tally to twenty-five. Oh, God, his forearms and fingers ached when he was through. He stood up and shook his arms to loosen them. Good. Should he answer mail or read a book? Every mail call brought a stack of letters. This morning he didn't feel like it. A pistol meant for him was inside the walls. The initial exultation was now tinged with something like fear. No, it wasn't fear.

From the front came the click-clack of the locking device being turned, followed by a key turning a cell lock. Bartlett, one of two white convicts on the tier, was coming out to shower and exercise for an hour, which consisted of walking up and down the tier, one man at a time. Men on this half of the bottom never went to the small yard. They were in super maximum custody. Those on the second floor, a mixed bag of convicts, went outside. The top floor did not. It was Condemned Row #2. Bartlett resided in the first cell, and the shower was next to that, so a guard standing outside the grille could look in at an angle, or through a small observation window in the wall. Bartlett was forty something, which made him an old timer in a world where the average age was twenty-three. Crime and prison were games for young men. He was awaiting trial for bribing a guard to bring him drugs.

Reading didn't work. His mind refused to concentrate. Other thoughts pushed out the words, and the page might as well have been in Sanskrit. Maybe he could write a letter. He picked up the pile of letters he needed to answer. He received as much mail as everyone else put together, much of it religious, Christians wanting to save his soul by leading him to Christ. He discarded most of them after a paragraph or two. Some contained religious tracts, or a stamped envelope. Others sent him a few dollars. The prison censors confiscated any letter sympathetic to revolution, although a few got through proclaiming *power to the people*, the catchphrase of the moment. He knew there were sympathizers out there. Whenever they went to court in San Francisco, the streets nearby and the building corridors were flooded with erstwhile warriors, and the lawyers forwarded letters that arrived from around the world. The prison could open letters for contraband, but could not read nor interfere with anything written from a lawyer.

The news that reached Eddie deep in the bowels of San Quentin was a distortion of reality, so he really believed revolution was underway. The bombs exploding on university campuses, American cities burning in the hot summers, these were all he saw from his worm's eye view, just enough to support his delusion that *Amerika* was being overthrown by the colored peoples inside and outside.

Paul Johnson, his sixteen-year-old brother, called "Boo" by both Eddie and Catherine, the oldest sibling, had been first in the visiting room. He was seated at the long table with the chin-high partition for almost an hour, looking at the entrance door whenever it started to open. The visiting room was half full, there was a buzz of conversation, and still no Eddie. It always took them a long time to deliver Eddie. He needed two guards for escorts, and they were not always available because of other duties, or so he had been told when he made enquiries.

Finally, he came through the door. Boo smiled. His big brother managed to swagger even in handcuffs. He sat down on the bench across from Boo. "What's shakin', Boo?"

"Nuttin' but the trees," Paul Johnson replied. "How you doin'?"

"Tryin' to stay strong in the belly of the beast."

"If anybody can, you can. Your book is doing good?"

"Yeah . . . but they edited it and made it less revolutionary than I wanted it, y'know what I mean?"

"I can dig it. When I read it, I thought, Man, this is my brother, but it ain't all of Eddie."

"I'm starting another one . . . not letters, but what I really wanna say about overthrowing this fascist mess that runs things and keeps colored people down on the bottom. Whoever controls the means of production controls everything.

"I'm not a *bona fide* Marxist scholar. I've been reading what I can get for about five or six years – and I know a few things. I'm a follower of Chairman Mao. You know what he said . . . ?"

Paul shook his head.

"He said to be scared of the dragon when the prison gates open."

Paul nodded. "Oh yeah! I know where he's comin' from."

"You get that book I recommended?"

"Which one? You tell me to read so many."

"The one by Debray, about urban guerrilla war?"

"The book store ordered it for me."

"Did Jimmy C call you?"

"The day after he got out. He'll be in the courtroom for you."

Eddie nodded with a smile on his face.

"That's not the trial, is it?"

"Just for hearing motions."

"How long you goin' to let this show trial go on?"

"Next week. All the world's media will be there."

"I know," Paul leaned closer and lowered his voice, simultaneously brushing his mouth so nobody could read his lips if they were trying. "I'm ready to make that move for you and whoever is with you. I got a fuckin' arsenal of guns."

"Where'd you get 'em?"

"Better you don't know."

"You didn't tell my lawyer? I don't want her around when things go down."

"No. Hell no! Like I know about givin' her some cover. She don't need to know. We got to figure a way for her to stay home that day."

"I'm tellin' Willy to be ready. You don't have a signal I can give him?"

"Man, when he checks me out in the audience, he'll know to be ready, 'cause the shit is comin' down any minute."

"You're more than a kid brother," Eddie said slowly, nodding his head for further affirmation. "You done become a *comrade*."

"Come on with that, Big Brother."

"We gonna change things a *little bit, a little, little bit*, and when we fall, we leave our sword for someone to pick up."

When Paul stood up to leave, the correctional officer phoned the Yard Office and asked for two escorts. Paul went out and raising a clenched fist, "Power to the People," he said, looking back – but he was a foot from the visiting room guard, at the exit door.

Eddie went the other way, into an alcove about three feet long; then there was a solid steel door with a permanently fogged observation window. He knocked, still in handcuffs, and the old guard working between the gates peered through the window and unlocked the door. He was along in between the gates, but at the front exit gate were two or three guards behind steel straps that served as bars. Along both side-walls were benches bolted to the walls. Often it was empty, or nearly so, which is how he found it. The old guard motioned with a forefinger toward the bench on the other side of the corridor. It was next to a small *pissoir*. It ended at the knees and the shoulders. It only had a urinal. This was an all-male prison.

The old guard looked through the small window to the Garden Beautiful inside the prison. The escorts were ten seconds away. "C'mon, Eddie. Your bodyguards are here."

He stood up wearing handcuffs, as the old guard opened the inner steel door and one of the escorts stuck his head in. "Ready, Eddie?" his reply was a nod and a step through the heavy steel gate into the bright warm sunlight. He momentarily closed his eyes and mentally photographed the scene and the sensations.

"Move on, Eddie," the lead escort said from behind.

He walked head up, chest out, conscious that convicts were watching him from the second and third floor windows of the Adjustment

Center – and from the crowd outside the chapel off to the right beyond the fishpond. He remembered some convict stealing a baby alligator from the education building and dropping it in the fishpond. Albert, the homicidal maniac (he wiped out his family) assigned to care for the fishpond went out of his mind. Convicts stayed away from the fishpond for a week. Albert was eyeing everyone suspiciously – and nobody wanted to be Albert's chief suspect, and probably the 'gator's dessert. The memory was funny and Eddie choked back a laugh. The guards would think he was laughing at them.

The Adjustment Center was a three-storey building on the left. The door was at the far end. The Adjustment Center was next to a redwood structure reminiscent of a smallish hot dog stand or coffee shop. It was the Yard Office, with glass walls so that people outside could look into the lieutenant's office at the rear. The building that preceded this one had a back room notorious for the out-of-sight beatings that frequently occurred there.

As often happened when Eddie returned from a visit, a white convict, about forty years old and elderly for prison, was seated with a book on a window ledge across the asphalt road from the Yard Office. He always looked up, watching Eddie cross the last thirty yards to the Adjustment Center door. They looked at each other and both gave the slight nod of acknowledgement. They reached the Adjustment Center door and an escort pushed the bell.

"Who's that convict back there?"

"Which one?"

"That white guy who is always reading right there?"

"That's Jimmy Farr. Yard Office Clerk."

The AC door opened and Eddie was ushered in. Now he had to strip for a skin search.

***

The shadows moving across the concrete floor could tell the approximate time of day. When the shadows crossed a crack in the concrete, the food cart was due. When the front gate opened, Eddie began doing four sets of twenty-five push-ups, as the food cart moved from cell to cell. Eddie finished both the push-ups and the meal by the time the cart reached the last cage and came back to the front on the way out. It would go to the cages on the other side, where the militant whites and *chicanos* were locked up next to each other. There were no hostilities between them. Many knew each other from the vast interlocked *barrios* of East Los Angeles where they lived side-by-side. They even wore identical tattoos from the same street gangs: White Fence, Hazard, El Hoyo Mara, Tortilla Flats, Clanton, Temple Street and dozens more. Lately they follow the blacks in the formation of a super-gang that superseded all the others.

He could hear the unique sound of spoons scraping the last scraps of food. Scott called out, "Hey, Eddie, wha's up, man? Was that youngblood come to see you?"

"Yeah."

Willy Easter was far down the tier. "Scott," he said, "ask Eddie if 'blood had a message for me."

"Tell him yeah. Everything is all right," Eddie called.

"I heard him," said Willy. "I'll run it by him tomorrow when I get out to shower."

"Tell him that's cool," Eddie called.

"Eddie says that's cool," Scott relayed.

"Right on! Right on! Right on!" he said excitedly, imagining his moment a few days away. Someone in an adjacent cell would have heard him snorting and grunting as he shadowboxed with the same slippery grace as when he danced. He'd come through the gate at age twenty, having been caught taking someone's El Dorado by looking mean and asking for it. Now he remembered and grinned. He sure did put white folks off their feed.

Willy heard the front gate open one cell away. He looked between the bars and saw the young bull (what the old timer convicts called them) coming in with the "clicker" to count the bodies one by one, and distribute an armload of mail.

"Hey, Eddie!" Willy yelled, "you got another *bag* of mail on the way."

Willy got one letter, from his lawyer, and the other cells got from none to four. Eddie had thirteen letters and everyone thought it was hilarious.

Except Spotlight Edison in the last cell; #17. "I'll be a dirty motherfucker," he cursed vehemently. "You got fifty bitches writing you goat mail. Me, I ain't got shit. If they killed and buried me under this big greasy motherfucker, ain't nobody would ever ask one damn question about where I was."

"Quit snivelin', punk," Eddie retorted. "You're with me in the revolution."

"Revolution! Shit! They got us buried in this fucker. They wanna send us to the gas chamber . . . especially you, Eddie."

"Leave me alone. I'm reading my mail."

"You get anything from Angel?" That was the nickname both had given to the beautiful young black woman who had appeared frequently in the courtroom; always smiling at Eddie.

His answer was a grunt. He was immersed in Angel's words:

" . . . had never seen a black man in chains until I saw you stand in front of that white judge, white district attorney, white lawyers, white cops, and almost all white people in the audience. You stood tall and proud as a king, or Jesus. I wanted to stand beside you and face the world as one. Rest assured that you will have support on the next appearance. Power to the People. A . . . "

He read it twice and put it over his face, savoring her odor. Although he would never admit it to anyone, he had never made love to a woman. There had been a gangbang on a stupid girl who had ventured down the wrong alley in the neighborhood to get drugs, but Eddie's reaction was disgust rather than arousal. He stopped the others and, in fact, helped the girl straighten her clothes before taking her almost home. He didn't go to the door for obvious reasons.

From the front came the sound of the cell control box being opened and a door opening, "Exercise, one hour, McGinnis!"

"That be me, boss man. Comin' on out."

The cell gate slid shut, followed by the rattle of the control panel and the spraying shower water. Eddie had heard it all.

With the background sound of the shower, he finished going through his mail. When the shower stopped, McGinnis appeared outside the gate. "Hey now, Eddie."

"Wha's up, homes?"

"I need a favor. An important one. I need you to call me as a witness. I need to see someone in court."

"Can you tell me what's so important?"

"I gotta get to the pay phone in the bullpen and call my old lady. She done got herself knocked up and thinks I'll hate the baby. She's planning on getting an abortion. We ain't married, so they won't let her visit me. Fuck all that. They be killin' too many black babies all around the world."

"Yeah. No bullshit about that."

Later, the guard rattled the cell gate from the control box in front and called out, "Shower and exercise, Johnson!"

"Rack it. Comin' out."

The cell gate slid out on rollers. He stepped onto the tier, wearing shorts, shower thongs and a towel draped around his neck. He swaggered along the cells, giving each some salute or wink. At

Willy's gate he stopped and leaned close to the bars, ignoring the guard who immediately called for him to keep moving.

"Add McGinnis to the list," he told Easter.

"Ahh, man, I dunno if I can."

"You can. Just do it. If the lawyer won't go for it, you tell the judge that it is necessary."

The guard began banging the bars of the front gate.

He went into the first cell, which had been converted to a shower. He disappeared into the steam rolling out.

It was Willy Dupree's trial day. Eddie was being taken to court with him as a potential witness. All hell had broken loose the day before, when the smuggled pistol had been discovered by a white prisoner on garbage detail. Seeing it as a sure ticket out of prison, the con turned it into the first bull in sight, not knowing that it had been Eddie's ticket out of jail.

He'd told Willy to look for Paul's signal. If this was the day they would be breaking out he did not want them to leave him behind in the holding cell.

The security in the move to the courthouse was extraordinarily tight. Scott was coming to court, too. He was Willy's alibi.

When the motorcade left the prison, a bystander might have thought that the Governor or the President was passing through. Two police cars with lights and sirens blaring led the way followed by three cars filled with armed guards with screened off back seats, each of the three carrying one prisoner. Bringing up the rear was another carload of guards and a roving motorcycle that kept other cars from passing or cutting in. When the convoy reached the courthouse, it was met by a crowd of boisterous protestors, some carrying signs, all loud and pugnacious, cheering loudly as each prisoner was taken from the vehicle and hustled into the building.

It was always tense, with glaring eyes watching the defendants being brought to the courtroom. And the trial hadn't even begun. This step was for motions to be argued. Both Scott and Willy refused the deputy public defenders, arguing that they were facing the death penalty, and there were lawyers who wanted to represent them pro bono. And Sally Goldberg had Eddie's case. It was chaos, but it was ultimately tight.

Where Willy Dupree's trial was being held, there were some cells, a bullpen and three armed bailiffs in addition to the correctional officers. The lead officer had a pistol. The others had 'gas billies', little clubs that also blasted forth tear gas. Hit with the gas a few feet away, you were through for the day. It wouldn't kill you, or permanently blind you, but for the rest of the day you were *hors de combat.* After decades of total control, there was an undercurrent of relaxation. Most of the guards were older men, because this was pretty easy duty. This wasn't a case of double murder with a hundred and four stab wounds, some right through the eye sockets. Willy Easter had simply gone nuts. He'd been a model prisoner until that morning. Officer Murchison described it very simply; "I was standing at the end of the number one steamtable in the North Dining Room. The inmates were filing along the steamtable, holding out their trays for the inmate servers to put a correct portion into the proper compartment. As I recall, they were having cinnamon rolls and peanut butter.

"I noticed this gentleman as he picked up his tray and spoon at the very start of the serving line. . . . He was eyeballing me in a hostile manner. I'm kind of accustomed to it. I mean San Quentin isn't all that cuddly, y'know what I mean?

"Anyway, I glanced at him again. He'd just gotten the roll, the peanut butter was coming, then the dipper of milk. I was at the end, supervising, so some convict wouldn't reach over and grab a score of rolls.

"He, that guy, he ain't looking at the rolls. He's still burning me. I see he's got the tray in both hands – some do that, but most use just one hand. It looks awkward. The instant he tensed, I broke and ran. He was cutting at my ass. We went down the aisle between the long tables, the old ones where everyone faced in one direction. Then I jumped up on top and ran about two steps before a foot came down on a tray and went out from under me. My feet went up, my ass and back came down, and I slid the length of the table on food trays. I was a mess when I came off the other end. The convicts were laughing, I was running and this guy was in hot pursuit with a big shiv, probably an old file that had been honed or ground down to a point.

"I got by him and ran flat out into the kitchen. He chased me around the big kettles, everybody got out of the way, until Lieutenant Seemen and Sergeant Snellgrove arrived and teargassed him.

"No, I have no idea why he picked me out. I'd seen him around the prison, but I can't recall any previous conversation or confrontation with him . . . "

The spectator benches were empty as a precaution against Eddie's appearance. The judge did not want Willy's trial to turn into what Eddie's was becoming – a trial in front of the world's media.

In the parking lot, a tall, slender black youth exited a yellow rental van and, carrying a heavily-laden paper shopping bag, entered the courthouse from the side entrance. There would be metal detectors at all courthouses after this day. The corridor was empty save for lawyers and other interested parties huddled with cigarettes outside one of the four courtroom doors. That wasn't the trial in which he was interested.

He looked through the small observation window in the next door and saw a correctional officer coming up the aisle toward the double entrance doors. He stepped aside. The door was pushed open and the prison guard walked past him. The black youth entered as the officer on the witness stand was being told that he was finished testifying for the morning.

The Judge said, "However you are still under subpoena and oath and should remain available to the process until the court dismisses you. Do you understand?"

"Yes, sir. I stick around in case somebody wants me."

"Precisely . . . " the Judge looked up over the courtroom. "This trial is in recess until one-thirty this afternoon." He punctuated the pronouncement with the gavel.

The young black man was Eddie's brother, Boo. He stepped into the aisle and extracted a short-barreled Israeli Uzi from the bag.

"All right, gentlemen, I am taking over." He swept the uzi over the Bailiff standing inside the courtroom door. "Come up to the front where I can watch you."

The Bailiff was a retired serviceman who augmented his pension with the income from this courtroom job. He wanted no trouble with this angry young black with the automatic rifle. The Bailiff walked down the aisle, hands above his head, and pushed through the swinging rail to the front. The other Bailiff was frozen beside the door into the bullpen, where the inmates were. They were pounding on the door while yelling: "Rack it, man! Open this fucker! C'mon, brother! Let us out."

Boo yelled to release the prisoners. The Bailiff unlocked the door and Eddie and Scott ran into the courtroom. One armed courtroom officer had his gun grabbed by Eddie.

"No one dies," said Eddie, taking over from his brother. "We are all going to walk out of this courtroom, quietly. Peacefully."

He ordered the judge to come down off the bench and to lead the parade. Flanking both sides of the three convicts were the court stenographer, the Bailiff and the two now unarmed court officers. Around the neck of the judge, Boo taped a short barrel shotgun.

The door to the cells was locked from the countryside but, as the group left the courtroom, officers on the other side started banging on the doors and alerting all the cops in the city that a massive jailbreak was under way.

The group of hostages now included the young district attorney and two more police officers found in the hallways. As the group entered the elevator, the DA said to the almost silent group, "You know you'll never get away with this. There'll be a whole army waiting for you outside."

"Shut the fuck up, or die now," said Eddie. "We cons will die here with guns in our hands, like men. What do you want to die for?"

As the elevator slowly descended, Boo started to speak, but was silenced by a look from his brother.

When they reached the lobby, it was crawling with cops, all with their guns pointed at them.

"Clear the lobby," Eddie shouted, "or we start killing hostages; the judge first. We want a van out front with the motor running. A van big enough for all of us. In five minutes, or someone dies."

The police shrank away, out the door. "Don't shoot anyone," said a high ranking cop, the last out the door. "We'll get your van."

The heat in the lobby was oppressive. The hostages, as well as the cons, were straining to breathe. The wait was torture.

"Everyone stay cool as we go out the door and we will all live. If any one of you hostages tries to make a break for it, I will kill you and all the rest. Listen to me, and we will make it. We'll drop all of the hostages as soon as we are in the clear."

In a few minutes the same police officer returned. "We have a red van waiting that can carry all of you. I have ordered the men not to fire, unless fired upon."

"Thank you, Captain," said Eddie politely. "Now lead the way, but stay close to the judge at the head of our parade."

As they exited the building, moving slowly, carefully, they could see, off to the side, that the only vehicle in sight was a red van under a tree, shaded from the hot sun. Nothing moved except loud, buzzing insects. Eddie jostled the judge. "Move it . . . toward that van," then to the other convicts, "Stay tight, don't give 'em a target. If they shoot, kill these motherfuckers.' He leaned closer to the judge's ear, "Hear that, honorable *Judge Denied*. That's your favorite word, ain't it? Denied! *Denied!* DENIED!"

Behind a low wall of shrubbery across the parking lot, the San Quentin guards and dozens of local cops sat on their butts, knees drawn up, rifles ready, the leather slings wrapped around their hands and wrists for stability. They had practiced for years for a situation like this – where they could shoot a scumbag con with absolute impunity. Their eyes were ice as they waited for the cluster of bodies to approach the red van. One guard leaned close to another. "When they open the door . . . "

The second guard nodded and wiped the sweat from his palms onto his pants. He was peering through the scope. At forty yards it was a point-blank shot.

Eddie squeezed to the front and pulled the van's door open. He turned his head. "Get in! Get in!"

Willy shoved the judge. "Go on." He did not know that the cross hairs were on the base of his skull. Indeed, he never knew, for the heavy lead slug tore through his skull into his brain. He ceased to be, but reflexes jerked the shotgun trigger and the judge's head became a grisly red spray with pieces of bone and brain splattering everywhere.

The other guard's shot was lost in the fusillade from eight officers. In seconds the van was perforated in dozens of places. Nobody knew if the convicts got off so much as a shot. When it was over, three were dead, including Eddie and his brother. The deputy district attorney was paralyzed from the waist down. By some miracle, none of the court officers were hit. Two of them broke loose and came running while a Marin County deputy was still firing, the heavy slugs making Willy's body jerk from the impact. The last hostage, the court stenographer, was under the judge's headless body and the deputy district attorney's limp legs. She screamed, "Stop! Stop! For God's sake, stop shooting!"

Afraid that Eddie was booby trapped with explosives, they had a long rope attached to his feet so they could drag him from the van while remaining at a safe distance. His body plopped onto the pavement. The image was caught by a television news camera and flashed all over America on the evening news. The Marin courthouse slaughter would be the impetus for the metal detectors, entrance guards and other manifestations of high security that permeate courthouses and other public buildings across the United States. Before, it was possible to walk freely in and out of courthouses and courtrooms without any security check.

Sally was in her car crossing the Bay Bridge from Oakland into San Francisco when she turned on the radio and it blared forth the news from the Marin Courthouse. At that point, the convicts and hostages were coming from the building toward the van. "They have the hostages in a tight group so only flashes of the convicts are exposed for seconds, not long enough to aim. The police are around corners and in doorways. When the convicts vacate a space, the police occupy it. They're close, but they can't do anything because of the hostages."

Knowing the layout of Marin Courthouse, Sally envisioned the drama from the announcer's words. She saw the parking lot and the van in her mind's eye. She knew that Eddie was at the courthouse for Willy's hearing.

The unexpected shot made her jump, and the following fusillade exploded in her brain. She knew it was a slaughter. Had Eddie survived? It made her queasy.

She slammed on the brakes, barely avoiding an accident.

When she got home, she was less doting than usual toward her children. The Nanny brought them down. She told them to go and play by themselves, then headed for the maid's room behind the kitchen. It had a small TV, which nobody would know she was watching.

Several channels had the scene live, with flashbacks to the action. The deputies were walking around the carnage. Flashbulbs popped, the voice said it was the bloodiest breakout attempt in decades. The image on the screen was that of a body with a rope around its leg. It was hauled unceremoniously out of the sliding side door of the van as if it was a side of beef. It landed without dignity on the pavement and seemed to bounce once. Sally's stomach rolled over and tears welled up in her eyes. She would never get to defend him in court. He'd died as he'd wanted to; with a gun in his hand. But the pictures on the TV made him look like an inert piece of meat. Not the hero she would have portrayed him as.

Sally switched the channel. "Christ almighty!" the image on screen was the same, the dead body being dragged from the van and bounced an inch or two on the pavement. "Oh God!" she cried softly but intensely, and shut off the television. A voice said the judge was dead, his head blown off by the shotgun taped around his neck.

Sally knew the judge. Like nearly all judges, he was biased toward the prosecution, but less than most. He was a good man who didn't deserve to die this way either.

That evening, in prisons all over America, black men mourned the loss of Eddie Johnson. He was gone, but would never be forgotten.

DEATH OF A RAT

A witness to the murder of the Soledad guard had been sent to San Quentin awaiting the trial. He was kept in the hospital's third floor. To reach him, you had to get through the hospital entrance by showing an identification card, with mug photo, name and number. Those details got you into the hospital Infirmary Room, normally used for treating cuts and dispensing cold pills. At the other side of this first room was a gate of steel bars painted white. A guard stood behind it, checking passes and identification. He had a board affixed to the wall with a hundred and fifty-two name tags, inmates who worked somewhere in the hospital, from laundry room to surgical nurse, clerk to the prison psychiatrist and the chief medical officer's clerk. Inmates who worked in the hospital wore green jumpers, which differentiated them from non-workers in blue chambray shirts.

A couple of weeks later the chief prison psychologist gave his clerk a list of men he wanted to see. The clerk dutifully typed up the list as a "request for interview". He put it on the psychologist's desk. It was signed and given back to the inmate clerk to be forwarded to the Custody Office, where the actual passes were made up and distributed throughout the cell-houses by the graveyard shift. This time, however, when the clerk got the signed list from his boss, he put it back in the Underwood and added two names and numbers, Clemens, B13566, and Buford, B14OO3. Both were young "fish", aged nineteen and twenty-two, and neither had been a year in the *House of Dracula*, the nickname for San Quentin. Folsom was *The Pit*, and Soledad *The Gladiator School*. Neither would admit it, but both wanted to be the stuff of legend in the prison underworld. During the night a guard walked the cell-house tiers, putting passes (called ducats) on the cell bars of convicts who were wanted somewhere by someone. Clemens was wide awake and waiting when the guard passed his cell. Buford got his when he woke up. They met on the Big Yard after breakfast. Neither had any appetite. Instead of hunger, both felt the hollowness of fear deep in the stomach. Normally they would have joined some partners hanging out in the morning sunlight near the North cell-house until the mess halls cleared and the whistle blew for work. This morning they wanted to hang out quietly until it was time to take care of business.

"Is that fuckin' whistle late this morning?" asked Buford.

Clemens shrugged. "I ain' got no fuckin' idea. I don' even know what fuckin' year it is."

The work whistle blasted the morning, causing an explosion of pigeons and seagulls. The latter flew over the yard and dropped their shit on the cons, as if getting vengeance for the whistle's blast. They were cursed in return. "Flying fuckin' rats," (in an attempt at retaliation, a few convicts would put Alka Seltzer tablets inside pieces of crushed up bread. The birds swooped, ate and soon went crazy as the Alka Seltzer fizzed inside of them).

The Big Yard gate was rolled open and convicts streamed out to their jobs in the lower yard industries. In minutes the yard was empty save for the cleanup crew and those who had night jobs. Lined up near the South Cell-house rotunda were those going to sick call.

A guard was picking up ID cards. When he reached Clemens and Buford, they showed the ducat and their ID cards. He beckoned them, "Follow me." The guard led them along the line to the Infirmary door. Because they had passes, they had priority over those who were in the sick call line on their own. He took their ID cards and put them with the others, to be returned when they left the hospital.

At the grille gate across the infirmary, they handed their passes through the bars. The guard keyed the gate. "You know where you're goin'?"

They nodded and he waved them through. The corridor ahead was long. A few inmates and free personnel were coming and going. The Psychiatric Department was halfway down the hallway. Instead of turning through the door, they kept going to the rear. On the left was an elevator. Inmates used it if they were patients or assigned. Others went up the stairwell, which was the route taken by Buford and Clemens, two and three stairs at a time. On the second floor they turned in and went to the X-ray department. They swiftly removed their shirts and tossed them under a bench. Now they wore the green jumpers. Anyone who didn't know better would assume that they were assigned to the hospital work crew. Clemens slapped Buford on the back. "Let's do it, homes." He opened the hallway door and out they went.

As they reached the third floor landing and started to turn in, an elderly correctional officer came out and nearly collided with them. "Slow down. Where's the fire?"

"Sorry, boss," said Buford. "We're late." If the guard had asked "For what," there would have been no reply, although Clemens' sweaty hand held the taped handle of the shiv in his pocket. It was a 15" long overall of which the tip of the blade had been stabbed through the bottom of his pocket and the steel pressed against his thigh.

"Okay, go on . . . just take it easy," the guard told them before disappearing down the stairs. They went through the door; to the left were the rooms. It was cleanup time and the doors were ajar. A *chicano* janitor was squeezing a wet mop in a wheeled bucket and wringer. The first door was into the nurse's station. It was open; the nurse was inside.

"Where's the rat?" Clemens asked Buford.

"At the back . . . around the corner."

"How we gonna get by the nurse?"

"That's what these green shirts are for."

"Let's go do him up."

They walked past the nurse's office without a challenge, and nodded at the *chicano* mopping the floors. Men in the rooms, mostly wearing nightgowns and jeans, glanced up as they went by, but suspected nothing and said nothing. With every step Clemens' tension increased. When they turned the corner and saw the correctional officer reading a newspaper, Clemens got momentarily dizzy. He expelled a lung-full of air.

The officer sensed, or heard them as soon as they turned the corner. The way they moved made him stand up and put the paper down. He saw the green blouses, but the hallway was a dead end ten feet away.

"Hold it. Where're you going?"

Clemens literally lost his mind. The tension was too heavy and he snapped. "Gimme them motherfuckin' keys, pig!" He didn't wait for the response, but pulled his shiv and stuck it straight into the officer's stomach, an inch below the rib cage.

"AhhhhhAHHHHH. God!"

Buford stepped forward and put a hand over Clemens' chest. "Cool it," and to the officer: "Better be givin' up them keys."

"I don't have them," he said, blood spraying out of his mouth.

In the cell, the witness, a black queen, heard the officer bang his back on the door when Clemens stabbed him. The queen got up to look through the observation window. She saw what was going on and ran to the window overlooking the air-well at the center of the building – and began screaming: "*HELP HELP HELP MURDER! OH GOD HELP!*"

From nearby windows came responding voices, but not of help. "Shaddup you ding bat motherfucker!" "Shut the fuck up, dick sucker, snitchin' nigger."

In the hallway, Clemens and Buford had the guard seated in the chair. Unable to resist, blood flowed from his mouth and down his shirt. He held his belly and hunkered forward. "Don't have keys," he said.

"Yeah . . . yeah," Buford was turning the guard's pockets inside out. Nothing.

Unexpectedly, the female nurse in white uniform came around the corner. She took a couple of steps before she realized what was going on. She turned and ran, with Buford in hot pursuit. Patients were sticking out their heads, but on seeing the nurse running and yelling they stepped back and closed the door. When they were questioned, and they would be, they would give the standard convict answer: "I didn't see nuthin', I didn't hear nuthin' – and I don't know nuthin'."

The nurse's office had a panic button, but Buford and his shiv were too close behind for her to turn in there. Instead she hit the stairway door and went through on the fly, screaming "*HELP*! *HELP*! *HELP*!" as she leaped, fell and rolled down the stairs, miraculously not breaking any bones and still screaming at the top of her lungs.

As Buford started down the stairway, his will ran out and fear filled him, sapping his strength. The nurse hit the first floor and ran into the main corridor.

Clemens came up behind Buford. "Did she get away?"

"Yeah, yeah. What're we gonna do?"

"C'mon!"

Clemens led the way to the second floor and turned in. "Best pray right here."

"Pray. What the fuck . . . !"

"Yeah, pray they pass on by to the third floor."

They heard the pounding feet and excited voices. "Go . . . go . . . on three." Four officers bounded past to the third floor.

Wordlessly, Clemens pulled Buford's sleeve and led him out of the second floor and down to the first. The main corridor had a dozen or more convicts looking toward the door into the stairwell and buzzing.

The corridor was long. The exit door was beyond the barred gate and infirmary. "Suck it up, dawg, an' let's go," he said then started walking with Buford on his heels.

The elderly guard on the barred gate was arguing with convicts on the other side. " . . . gonna want us," the convict said. "We're the surgery crew. They've been calling us on the loudspeaker. Here –'He brought out a yellow 'Assignment Card'. It said *'Hospital – Surgery'*."

"Wait," said the guard as he picked up the phone and checked with Control, holding down his voice. "Stand aside. When they need you they'll call." At the same moment, he looked back over his shoulder to Clemens and Buford in their green hospital worker blouses. The guard nodded and turned the key in the barred gate. Buford and Clemens slipped out into the Big Yard.

"LOCKUP! LOCKUP!" blasted the public address system. Convicts looked at one another, shrugged and began to slowly file into the vast cell-houses.

In the dark hours before dawn, the sound of boots crunching, and tall shadows made by prison floodlights, gave notice that guards were on the tiers. They took Buford first and went back for Clemens. On the way down the rear steel stairs, the night-sticks rose and descended. One blow gave off the hollow sound similar to that of a breaking egg. It was actually Clemens breaking his skull. He was in a coma for a week, and would be a mumbling idiot for the rest of his life. That saved Buford, for the guards were afraid of what they had done. Their reports said he had fallen down the steel stairs to the concrete floor.

The sun was rising and the baby pigeons and other birds were making an inordinate ruckus that most convicts slept through when Buford was walked across the prison to the Adjustment Center. There was the bang and slam of gates opening and being shut until they got him into a cell on the bottom floor of the north side of the AC, a collection of around half a dozen men the officials thought were the most dangerous in the entire prison system of sixty-eight thousand.

DEATH ROW BREAKOUT

He had been waiting for the verdict that would mean death. There could be no other verdict. This was the end of the road, and Roger knew it. He'd been eyeing the jurors for weeks. The blacks would convict him for the deaths of the black preacher and his wife. The whites would nail him for the murder of a white cop. Never mind that he'd been stopped at a roadblock with his two hostages, and that it was the shots of the cops that had set his car on fire. The preacher and his wife were dead. He'd then shot the cop who had come up to the blazing car and was about to kill him, as he lay wounded and trapped behind the wheel. Who would believe that an ex-con could shoot a cop in "self-defense"? No one. He could see that in the jurors' eyes as they glared at him.

The prosecuting attorney had portrayed Roger as some kind of mad dog. And what does society do with a Mad Dog? That was what his partner was called, and he had had to kill him, as well. He'd made some mistakes along the way, but he was not insane. If he had one major failing, it was that he could not resist the adrenalin charge of the good caper. He'd studied that bank for weeks and had almost gotten away with the cash until his car broke down. The kind minister had stopped to give him a lift. And all it had gotten him and his wife was a fiery end. For that, Roger was sorry. For the cop, he was not.

They'd called him and his sorry-assed defense attorney back into the courtroom for the verdict. All rose as the judge entered. The jury had found him guilty. This was the penalty phase. Was it going to be life imprisonment? He'd be out in 25 years, if lucky. Or was it death?

The judge's voice was a rolling chant, like a priest saying mass: " . . . the jury having found you guilty of violating Section 187, California Penal Code, murder, and having found special circumstances and having set the penalty of death, this court finds no reason to set aside such verdict.

"Therefore, it is the Order, Judgement and Decree of this Court that you, Roger Nellis Harper, be delivered to the custody of the Warden of the California State Prison at San Quentin, where you will be put to death at a time and in a manner prescribed by law."

"The execution of the Death Warrant is herewith stayed pending automatic appellate review."

"Defendant is remanded. The case is closed. Court is adjourned – and may God have mercy on your soul."

The gavel descended, the bailiffs closed around Roger, and he watched the judge move from the bench. How huge he was up there in his robes, how human and puny when stripped of his office.

"See you at the jail," said the appointed lawyer, but he never did. He waved at Roger while leaving the courtroom. Roger saw the absurdity and laughed.

Four nights later, after midnight when the shift changed, he heard the rattling chains and knew they had come for him. An hour later, following paperwork and processing, they took him the back way to a three-car caravan. He was draped in more chains than a Christmas tree has tinsel, including leg-irons. Deputies with riot guns were abundant and, when Roger looked up, he saw a couple silhouetted against the night sky. There was an aura of tension, as if they half expected an attempt at armed rescue. It made Roger chuckle as he got into the rear of the station wagon. Some lying stoolpigeon had told gullible authorities that he was the Aryan Brotherhood's "hit man" hired to an international drug cartel. The Sheriff's Department had an appetite for such stories. Such threats required greater resources, bureaucracy grew. The truth was that few were the fools *loco* enough to attack even two armed deputies to rescue a friend. It was too likely that everyone would bite the dust, including the friend.

The caravan rolled. First the black and white with flashing lights and four deputies. Then the station wagon with Roger in a rear compartment and two deputies in front. Finally another black and white with four more deputies behind.

When they reached the highway, the lead car turned off the flashing lights and the caravan rolled north through darkness toward San Quentin's death house.

Twenty minutes out, the Interstate crossed the State highway where the murderous battle had occurred. Without that night's fog, it was open rich farmland. The blazing exchange was relived in his brain. He'd been violence hardened in reform school where boys fought every day. He remembered a counselor killing a boy by twisting a towel around his neck. Leaving no mark, it cut off blood to the brain. The man never lost a day's wages. So Roger knew then that was the way the world was – and so it was. He'd seen two teenage *chicanos* stab each other to death. One fell dead at the scene, the other merely reached the hospital before his heart filled with blood. He died on the spot. Roger also saw a cop shoot a fourteen-year-old *chicano* off a fence, the boy silhouetted like a clay pigeon on the lighter ink of the night sky. They said he had a weapon and the inquest justified the killing. Yes, Roger was hardened to violence early on. Alas, that had not applied to Sidney and Florence. Over and over he remembered the wounded cop emptying his weapon, through the back of the car, and every time he saw it in his mind's eye, he felt weak and queasy and, sometimes at night in the cell, tears came to his eyes. He'd known them only a few hours; it was long enough to feel their simple Christian goodness. Now they were dead and he was sentenced to die for their murder. For the deputy with the shotgun, who had fallen backward, wounded in the neck, and had drowned in the irrigation ditch, Roger had been sentenced a second time to Life Without Parole. The deputy's death was tragic, but it was part of the game in Roger's mind. The officer was paid to carry a gun and shoot people when necessary. If there was to be no risk, why give him the gun? Society vilified him, but he despised society and didn't care what people thought. A surrender would have brought a razzing from his pals. A true hardcore never stained the flag by throwing down the gun.

San Quentin, home of Condemned Row, is a sprawling mass of concrete and steel on a peninsula in Marin County, overlooking an extension of San Francisco Bay. It began when a Spanish prison ship ran aground. A plank was extended to shore, a building was erected, then another and another. Over time, these were torn down to be replaced by others, evolving into a community dominated by four giant cell-houses with fortress-thick walls, plus sundry auxiliary buildings. The South Cell-house was the largest in the world, a thousand cells housing two thousand numbered men. Condemned Row #1, however, was in the North Cell-house. Actually, it occupied a separate floor on top of the cell-house. That made it convenient to reach the two 'overnight condemned cells' and the gas chamber behind the North Cell-house. In recent years, so many men had been sentenced to death that Death Row overflowed the top floor of the North Cell-house and filled two floors of the Adjustment Center, creating Condemned Row #2 and #3.

It was first light when the three-car caravan crossed the Richmond-San Rafael Bridge with the prison visible on the other side. Stars were fading into the morning. They were likely to be the last stars he would ever see. For a terrible moment he confronted the truth of death, of oblivion, of not *being*. His heart began to race. The vision was blinding, too much for the mind to contain. Non-being was not sleep.

The outer gate opened. The road ran along the shoreline to another gate. The two escort cars pulled to the side. Only the station wagon with the condemned man went through the second gate. It pulled up to the East Sallyport; the pedestrian gate into the main security area. Less than a year earlier, Roger had walked out the other way. On both days the sun was bright on the bay.

In Receiving and Release, the same grizzled Sergeant was in charge, and Roger recognized the inmate clerk. The other convict was new. He was probably a Lifer to have the job. He had the look of a wife killer – one crime; one time. Roger was fingerprinted, photographed and given a Condemned Row issue. It was the same as that given to mainline convicts except there were no razor blades, no web belt and, instead of heavy brogans, they issued his soft-soled slippers. The Sergeant was indifferent, and the convicts maintained a psychological distance. Death Row was a world removed from the rest of San Quentin. It had some communication with the mainline via tier tenders and a convict clerk; although they were skin searched coming and going, they could transport verbal messages – and things the right size could go in a 'keister plant', – up the rectum. Anything not metal would get through and, seeing as how drugs were the #1 item of desire, that was what they smuggled to those sentenced to die.

Meanwhile, in the Control Room, the Control Sergeant inserted the tag, Harper, Roger N., A20284B, in the slot on the board: Cell #C.R. 1/56. He reached for the phone and dialed Death Row. "Howdy Blair, got a dead man walkin' your way. A two or two eight four. Harper . . . goes into fifty-six. Got it?"

"We'll have it ready for him."

Roger, still in waist-chains but without leg-irons, walked behind a guard who cleared the way, calling out, "Dead man walking." It made convicts step far back. He'd seen it often from the sidelines; now he was the main attraction.

Behind him came a second guard and, on the catwalk along the outside of the cell-houses, was a rifleman with a carbine. They were more wary of some maniac on the mainline killing one of the condemned – someone like Sirhan, Ramirez or Manson – than that anyone would escape or do any damage. They were always in cuffs and waist-chains.

As they entered the big yard and turned left to walk along the length of the North Cell-house, Roger looked out across the yard, half of which was under a high weather shed, like a giant hay shed, and was always shaded and cool. The sun shone bright on the other half, and there were clusters of pigeons and several seagulls.

Convicts were few; none he knew. They stood expressionless as the retinue passed through.

At the North Cell-block entrance, the gun-rail ended. They stepped into the rotunda. An open door led into the cell-house; noise came out at them. Across the rotunda was a locked steel door. That way led to the elevator landing and a green steel door. Beyond that door were the overnight condemned cells, where the doomed were moved for the last night. Next to the cells was another door, beyond which was the green, octagon-shaped gas chamber. It was four steps from the overnight cells to oblivion. Last *mile*, my ass . . .

The sound of the elevator turned Roger's thoughts away from the green door. One of the escorts pulled the elevator door open. They got aboard and it rattled upward – to the floor above the North Cell-house.

They stepped onto a landing. A face peered through a tiny window in a door and identified them. Then came the sound of a big key being turned: the door opened. Beyond, waited a half circle of two correctional officers and a Sergeant, plus an armed guard in a gun cage providing backup.

Roger knew the Sergeant. His name was Blair and he'd worked in San Quentin for thirty years without writing a single disciplinary report. He had the seamed face of a happy old boozer. He looked at Roger and shook his head. "Sorry to see you like this, Harper. I thought you might make it out there."

Roger shrugged. "I fucked up."

"Nobody's perfect," said Blair.

While the Sergeant examined the paperwork, Roger looked through a small, double-gate sallyport onto a tier. Half a dozen condemned men were out of their cells. Two paced up and down, side-by-side, while the other four played bridge on the floor at the far end, using a blanket for a card table. Death Row was the only place in the prison that allowed card playing.

Roger recognized one of the walking men, Jellico by name. He had been a key clerk in the prison hospital who never caused any trouble. It was a complete surprise when he was paroled and went on a murder spree through Frisco's gay community. Using his last victim's credit cards, he went to Las Vegas and partied for over a week, until the credit cards led the police directly to him. They found a taped confession. When caught, he said, "Fine, I want the gas chamber. I'll do it again if you don't execute me." The jury obliged.

Roger recalled reading that Jellico had an execution date. As he had not read anything for over a month, the execution had to be imminent. The law required the death warrant to be executed between sixty and ninety days.

"Better lock 'em up while we run him in," Sergeant Blair said.

A guard banged a big key on a pipe. The sound rang out. "Okay, grab a hole in there."

The other guard unlocked a heavy padlock on a simple hydraulic handle. He pulled the lever, raising the heavy security bar above the tops of the gates. Each inmate pulled his gate open, stepped inside and shut it. When the tier was clear, the guard dropped the security bar. When the bar was down, the gates were blocked shut. Each gate also had its individual lock.

The catwalk guard opened the tiny sallyport gate, and the other guard entered. As he walked down the tier, locking individual cells, the armed guard on the catwalk walked beside him, giving him armed backup.

When he was sure each cell was locked individually, he signaled to the guard at the lever. The security bar was raised again. The guard on the tier unlocked the next to last cell, went inside and looked around, tossing the mattress and turning his flashlight beam into the vent at the rear. It was routine and fast; how long does it take to examine a bare concrete cage four and a half feet wide and eleven feet long?

He flashed the light down the tier. It was time to bring in the resident.

Roger, still encumbered by cuffs and waist restraint, carried his bedding down the tier. Two guards walked with him, and the gun-rail guard walked along beside them. Sergeant Blair waited at the front by the lever to the security bar.

As Roger walked, he looked at the faces of the doomed men in the cages. Some ignored him, others looked out with hard faces and the flat eyes of the cold-blooded killer, others with the fiery eyes of madmen. He would learn their names and their crimes as weeks went by, but for now he recognized just a few. For a moment he looked into the black eyes of Richard Romero, the "Hollywood Monster", the most notorious serial killer of the decade. He'd committed crimes so bestial and heinous that the press refused to print the details. A man who'd been in jail with Romero told Roger that the Monster had sodomized a year-old baby while cutting its throat.

Two cells from Romero a slender man stood at the bars with a grin. It was Jimmy Rube, half *chicano* member of the Mexican Mafia. Roger remembered Jimmy Rube as a handsome young man with wavy dark hair. Now the hair was thinning and grey, although the body was still slender and the face youthful. He'd served twenty-two years, and then, twenty-two days after being paroled, he and Big Strunk killed a store manager in West LA.

"Where's Big Strunk?" Roger asked as he passed Jimmy.

"Right here, man," called a voice ahead. Seconds later, Roger passed the squat black man whose powerful torso and immense arms were covered with blue, India Ink tattoos, the kind that denote jail just as surely as a missing finger on a Japanese denotes Yakuza.

Goddamn, there seemed to be a lot of mean-looking young niggers on Death Row.

The guard ahead held the cell gate open. Roger stepped inside. The gate closed; the security bar dropped in place; the key turned in the big door lock.

"Back up here," one ordered, then reached through and unfastened the waist chains. They rattled as they dropped to the floor.

Roger held his hands up to the bars and the handcuffs were removed. The other guards departed, but Sergeant Blair remained.

"Look, Harper, I don't expect trouble from you, but I'll tell you what I tell everyone.

"You know me and I think you know I try to treat everybody right. As long as you don't give me any grief, I'll do whatever I can to make things easy on you up here. God knows you've got enough troubles already.

"I make sure the food is hot when it gets here. They used to load the cart two hours before it came up the elevator.

"I make sure the library sends up the law books and, if they don't have them here, we get them from the State law library.

"I got authorization to let inmates out on the tier together if they can get along. So instead of getting half an hour every other day, most of you get a couple hours everyday."

Sergeant Blair leaned closer and lowered his voice, not wanting to be heard in the adjacent cells. "Have you got any enemies up here? Somebody you don't get along with?"

"No." Roger shook his head, his cheeks burning. It was true that he had no enemies – except that he loathed the Hollywood Monster – but even if he had a deadly enemy, he would never ask the man to keep him in his cell. That was one step from ratting on someone. He would have denied the fact if a mortal enemy was here. Of course, if it was two or three – with shivs . . .

"The tier tender will bring blankets and . . . uh . . . an earphone for the radio and TV. Take it easy." He patted the bars as a gesture of goodbye and turned away. The clang of the gate marked his leaving the cell area.

Roger looked around. The cell was identical to those on the mainline, four and a half feet wide, eleven feet long. The only differences were that it had one bunk instead of two, and the wall between cells extended out an extra foot so it was impossible to reach out of the bars and pass things by hand. The cell was so narrow that he could sit on the bunk with his back resting on one wall and his feet propped on the other. This would be his home for a decade or so, while he ran through the appeals process. First came the direct appeal, followed by a *Petition for Writ of Certiorari* to the United States Supreme Court. If the conviction and sentence were affirmed on the trial record, he still had the remedy of the Great Writ, *habeas corpus*, which he had to start in the State courts. He had to exhaust State remedies before the Federal District Court had jurisdiction. He could appeal from there to the United States Court of Appeal for the 9th Circuit and, finally, one last shot at the United States Supreme Court. When he reached there, they would be strapping him in the chair. The thought made him smile, but deep inside was a knot of fear.

From the clutter of sound, voices down the tier, gates opening and a typewriter's rattle on the other side, a closer voice called out, "Hey, Roger baby!"

"Is that you, Big Strunk?"

"That's me. Jimmy Rube says he's gonna send you some cigarettes and magazine and coffee when Fast Eddie comes in."

"Who's Fast Eddie?"

"The tier tender – old white dude with tattoos up the ass."

From a cell too distant for easy conversation, Jimmy Rube yelled, "I'll see you tomorrow when I come out to shower."

"I'll be right here, man."

"If you ain't, the count's gonna be fucked up."

Roger spent the rest of the day getting the feel of Death Row. He watched the little he could see through the cell bars, and listened to sounds and voices. The dinging bell brought the elevator, heralding the prison's Chief Nurse, a woman of fifty nicknamed Madam Chickenshit. She passed out medications, everything from aspirin to Thorazine, and cold pills to sleeping pills. The Chief Medical Officer was liberal with seconal. He hoped the guy killed himself. It saved the victim's family added pain. It saved money. It rid the world of someone who didn't deserve to live.

Madam Chickenshit stopped at Roger's cell and asked him if he had any medical problems. No. Then the doctor would give him a physical next week.

The dinging bell also brought the Watch Lieutenant, making a routine survey and signing a log. Everything had to be according to the book on Death Row. The bell also heralded the rattle and bang of the food cart. Death Row got two meals a day, one about eight-thirty in the morning, the other at three in the afternoon. Everything had to be locked tight from 4:00 pm to 8:00 am. It was absurd to serve three meals in eight hours to be finished before 4:00 pm. Everything was locked at the beginning of the third watch. Instead they got a bologna sandwich and an orange for a late-night snack and the third meal guaranteed by law.

Besides the dinging bell announcing the elevator, he usually heard the tier gate when someone entered. The angle on the mesh and bars of the gun-walk was such that he could see only a moving shadow until the gun guard was directly in front of his cell.

After 4:00 pm, the bell rang no more. The key to the outer door was taken off Death Row and kept in Wall Post #2, the gun tower over the Big Yard gate. If someone had to enter Death Row, the key was lowered in a bucket. At midnight it came down for the shift change.

At 6:00 pm, the television sets, one for each three cells, were turned on. The speakers had been cut off and the sound was delivered by tiny earphones, through wire too thin to hang oneself. Each of the three cells controlled the remote channel changer for a week at a time. Roger didn't give a rat's ass what they watched. He normally watched little television, but would watch more now. He'd been a reader since juvenile hall. Now he would read more, watch more TV . . . jack off more often, and think. What else was there to do on Death Row? At least it wasn't like the old days in France, where you never knew when they would come for you.

He turned off the cell light and lay in the semi-darkness. The runway lights, and floodlights on the roof of the immense cell-house, entered the cell after being sliced into linear shadows by cell bars, runway bars and wire, window bars, layer after layer of barrier to the outside night. It was air-tight. Escape crossed his mind. It always crossed his mind in a new cage. Here, however, a cursory catalogue of the security measures brought swift certainty that odds of escape were worse than rescue by the Second Coming. More likely America would have a revolution than he would escape from here.

He knew the obstacles from the years on the mainline. He'd thought about it then. The North Cell-house rotunda and the elevator were the only places where you weren't directly "under the gun" of an armed guard, looking down your throat. Before leaving the cell, you did the strip-search dance for the bulls, watching through the bars. They watched you put on the jumpsuit and hold your hands up to the bars so they could be cuffed in steel. The bulls barely put their fingers in until the handcuffs closed. Finally, you backed up and were wrapped in chains fastened to the cuffs and run up between your legs. If you made any kind of too-fast move, a jerk would throw you on your face. Because of the cuffs and chains you couldn't stop the collision with concrete. No, it was unlikely that the killer could overpower three bulls in the elevator. Bull – tough bulls – with clubs, pepper spray and radios to summon immediate help. *That* was the *weak* spot. As he thought it, he snorted a laugh.

Unless he managed to go out to a County Jail somewhere and from there escape – that was within the realm of possibility – this was where he would make his stand. Would he die like a man?

Again the terror flashed through him. He fought it, made himself breathe more quietly. Death came to everyone. His life expectancy was a minimum of six years. How many people would give everything for six more years – even in a cell?

Florence and her husband, the couple he'd kidnapped, came to mind. He could see them in the mirror again. It made him breathless. He would die for their murder. He would be willing to die if it could bring them back. No, that was a lie. But he would cut off an arm – and he goddamn sure would have surrendered, if he'd imagined his failing to do so would have cost their lives. He was legally responsible, and morally too – and yet . . . Maybe it was God's justice on him for killing his ex-partner, Mad Dog. That crazy thought also made him snort a laugh.

As if his laugh was a cue, a chorus of laughs issued along the tier. The murderers laughed. What the fuck was going on? Were they mocking him? Then he realized that they were all watching the same TV show and had laughed at what they'd seen.

A conversation from the cells near the front had been going on below the threshold of his attention, but suddenly he found himself plugging in.

"Nigger be akin' ovah in South Africa. Wish I was there man? 'stead'a this motherfucker."

"Yeah, man . . . If I was there, man, I be killin' soft-ass white motherfuckers . . . call themselves Africaners . . . like they be some parta Africa. Bullshit!"

"Yeah, dig up them that's dead and kill 'em again."

"When I raise from this muffucker, I'm goin' to Africa, man. No bullshit, man. I wanna get away from white people, man. I don't like 'em, man. I don't like their white skin, like dead white fish. Look at this beautiful brown skin . . . "

"When I look at whitey, man, I think, how could sissy-ass muffucker like this conquer the muffuckin' world, man. Y'know what I mean, nigger? Muffuckers can' bust a muffuckin' grape. They can' fight a lick. When a niggah run down on 'em dey be so scared . . . "

"Yeah, I can dig on that, man. It be fuckin' weird, man."

Roger closed his eyes, thinking, Oh god, do I gotta listen to these idiots for a decade? Should I say something? He managed an inner smile; he was sure they'd never heard a white man murder mouth like he would if he got started.

But the gates were locked. This was Death Row. It would be like animals in separate cages in the zoo, screaming primordial rage. If he got into it, he would probably have a stroke. It was so stupid anyway. What had they done to be sentenced to die? They must have some notoriety somewhere.

What about Big Strunk and Jimmy Rube? It was hard to conceive their allowing such Mau Mau bullshit for very long. Strunk was on Death Row for killing a stoolpigeon on a Department of Corrections bus. Strunk wrapped his chains around the man's neck. Guards on both ends went crazy. The driver swerved the bus back and forth. The gun guard couldn't use the shotgun. Nobody was escaping. Strunk wasn't known to take a lot of bullshit. Nor was Jimmy Rube. Roger had seen Rube stick a black convict prizefighter – tough with his fists – but he screamed like a woman when Jimmy Rube stuck that shiv under his ribcage. The shiv cut part of his heart. Miraculously (and because he was in such excellent condition) the sucker lived. He stopped snitching, too.

As if by telepathy, Roger heard Jimmy Rube's voice, "Hey, Bro', I'll run it by you in the *mañana* when I exercise."

"I got it, homes," he called back, and was quiet. Again he heard the chorus of laughter at the TV. The murderers had found something funny. Roseanne? Naw. Too near reality to be funny to convicts. Too ugly, too. They wanted to watch someone young and foxy swish around the screen.

After the night on the highway and the day being processed into Death Row, Roger was tired. When he heard the sound of convicts moving across the Big Yard, their voices floating up through the night air, he could close his eyes and see them walking along the white lines, watched by riflemen on catwalks. Roger knew the scene because he'd attended night school to prepare for his GED. A lot of good it had done him. Sleep embraced him. If he dreamed, he had no memory of it.

In the morning, after breakfast and cleanup, Sergeant Blair could be heard coming down the tier and calling out to someone, "Shower and exercise," and when he passed Roger without stopping, Roger called him back. "Sarge, what's up? Am I on cell status?"

"You gotta be classified. I don't know who to let you out with."

"Let me out with anybody."

"We don't do it that way – too much trouble. You'll probably be with Strunk and Rube and that kid."

Roger heard Sergeant Blair turn the key on one cell gate. As soon as he left the tier, the security bar went up.

A cell gate opened and closed.

A moment later, Richard Romero slithered past, flicking his eyes into each cell. He had a peculiar stride, with his ass under slung and his slippered feet sliding along the floor, that reminded Roger of a snake. Roger refused to acknowledge the maniac's existence. He had no fear of such monsters. Invariably they were cowards if the victim wasn't helpless. Fear was deeply involved in their crimes. They swam in it and derived great pleasure from inflicting it. If I could lay my hands on this motherfucker, Roger thought, envisioning smashing his fists into Romero's face – or taking a claw hammer to his head. To avoid looking at the monster and working himself up, Roger put on the earphones and closed his eyes, listening to the music on the prison radio.

Later, he heard a guard yell, "Romero, lock up." He heard the cell gate shut and the security bar go down, followed by the guard coming in, locking the cell gate and unlocking three others. The gates were still shut until the guard went out and lifted the bar. Then, gates came open and clanked shut. Roger "saw" it all in the sounds, which he understood from a lifetime of hearing similar noises.

Jimmy Rube and Strunk appeared outside the bars, both grinning. Strunk was shirtless and carried a towel and a soap dish. His skin was freckled, his chest immense, his arms gigantic. He had so many jailhouse tattoos that his body looked like a wall of graffiti. "Hey, my brother, I'm sorry to see your sorry old ass – but I can't talk to you right now. I gotta go shower. I'll be back. Talk to Rube. He's got shit to tell you."

"Okay, Muscles. See ya later. Rub oil on the fine body."

"Man, fuck you," Strunk said, turning away. Then stopped. "I've got some magazines down there. A stack of *New Yorkers*. You want 'em?"

"Yeah, sure, send 'em down."

Strunk nodded without turning, and went on down the tier.

Rube stepped forward; his eyes had a brightness at odds with the situation. "Sorry you're here, homeboy but . . . you wanna get out?"

Roger wondered if he'd heard right. "Come again?"

"Would you believe you got here in time to break out?"

Roger's heartbeat skipped as hope ignited – but a moment later the cynicism of reality made him dubious. "How's that gonna happen?"

Rube glanced over his shoulder to make sure the gun-walk guard was nowhere nearby. Rube lowered his voice. "We've cut the gun-walk bars and screen."

Could that be true? Yet even if it was true, where would they go? They were still on Death Row. "So what then?"

"Oh man, don't be so negative. It took us a motherfuckin' year to do it. Now we're about a week from cutting Strunk's bars. We take it real slow – when the TVs are on and suckers are talking – muffle the sound in soap and rags.

"Anyway, when Strunk can get out of his cell, we wait till the first watch, after midnight, he goes out there and snatches the gun-bull. The gun-bull can go through a gate out front. He grabs the Sergeant and the other bull.

"Outside the tier, there's that window on that side." Rube gestured to indicate where he meant.

"We cut the bars on the window and we're on the roof."

Roger could see the scene. That high window was above an outdoor gun-rail, and 10 feet below the roof of a building that housed the bachelor officers' quarters and radio room. On at least one occasion Roger knew of, a convict had climbed on the roof by the mess hall and then crawled right past this point. The roof here joined with the roof of the Custody Office and Inside Parole Office. At the corner, where the building ended, was a blind spot where the escaping convict got out unseen. But where then? They'd be captured trying to get across the Golden Gate Bridge. It was a long shot. But give a guy a long shot who was facing certain death – and he'd take it.

Rube was waiting, eyes aglow, grinning gleefully.

"It sounds like it's worth a try," Roger finally said.

Big Strunk reappeared, rubbing a towel through his wet hair with one hand and carrying a stack of *New Yorkers* with the other.

"Here you go, homeboy," he said, putting them on the bars.

"My turn to shower," Rube said.

"Yeah, go wash that funky body," Strunk said.

When Rube was gone, Strunk asked, "He tell you about it?"

"Yeah."

"What do you think?"

"It's a shot . . . maybe a long shot . . . but better'n sittin' around jackin' off."

A young man walked past behind Strunk. "Who's that?" Roger asked.

"That's Robillard." Strunk turned. "Hey, Robillard, come here."

The young man came back and Strunk introduced him. Roger thought he looked sixteen. Actually, he was nineteen. He'd been raised in a foster home. When he was eighteen, he graduated from foster care to the street on his own, poorly educated and untrained. Somebody offered him $500 to steal a car. He did so – and ten minutes later a Highway Patrolman turned the red light on him. It was Robillard's first crime, and he was terrified. When the Highway Patrolman walked up to him, Robillard shot him dead and was sentenced to die under the felony murder rule. After Robillard walked away, Strunk said, "He's scared. But what he's most scared of is that he'll piss his pants or break and have to be carried into the gas chamber."

"Shit, I worry about that, too," Roger said. "Don't you?"

"Man, I don't think about it. And when I do, I stop real quick and concentrate on this breakout working."

From the front they heard one of the black voices from the night before. It was loud, "Hey, motherfucker, get over here."

Strunk rolled his eyes to the skies and leaned back to look down the tier. "Those two fuckin' niggers. Damn!"

"What're they doin'?"

"Callin' Robillard over. They want him to pass something," Strunk raised a hand and waved, obviously getting Robillard's attention, and then signaling him to go along with the demand.

"I heard those fools last night," Roger said. "I was gonna say somethin' until Rube signaled me off."

"We can't do anything up here – but even if we started yellin', we could wind up getting a cell move over to the Adjustment Center, or around the other side. Wouldn't that be a bitch? Be ready to break out and they move you out of your cell, maybe to another building. With my luck, they'd put the nigger in my cell and he'd be the motherfucker to get out."

Robillard appeared behind Strunk. "What happened?" Strunk asked.

"He wanted me to carry something down the tier. I wasn't going to do it until you signaled me. I feel kinda sorry for the way black people been fucked over, but that's no reason to disrespect folks. Fuck him in his ass."

"Yeah . . . yeah . . . yeah – but we can't be that way right now."

"Hey, home," Strunk said to Roger, "I gotta get some exercise. I'm gonna walk some. You'll be out with us next week. Classification is Friday."

"They're gonna classify me, huh?"

"Yeah, minimum custody."

Strunk and Robillard passed back and forth a couple of times, eventually joined by Rube, who was fresh from the shower. He took a couple of turns, talking to them, and then came over to Roger's bars. "What happened? Those young niggers making you warm?"

"Not really, but, man, that shit could get old real fast. All that paranoid self-pity – plus all that murder mouth, offin' this motherfucker and that nigger, like it was a fuckin' movie they were in. Bein' baaad is cool."

"I don't know about that," Rube said, "but I do know they snitched on each other ten minutes into the police station . . . tryin' to get down first. There was a third guy, and he walked free because he didn't say a word except that he wanted a lawyer."

"What was the crime?"

"Brave deal. Out in Oakwood where the Mexicans were having a war with the Shoreline Crips, remember that?"

Roger nodded. It had been in the newspaper before he was paroled. In one square mile in a five-month period there had been forty shootings and a dozen deaths.

"They saw some young Mexican bopping along the street with his chick – so they drove by and opened up; spray and pray. They missed the guy, but they killed the girl and she was five months pregnant. They also got an old white woman in her house. She was the neighborhood nice lady. So they gave these two fools the death penalty under that new federal law."

"Anyway," Rube continued, "when they get on your nerves, before you open your mouth, remember that we might get outta here in a couple of weeks if you keep it shut."

"Yeah, you're right. If you can, I damn sure can."

"What're you sayin'?"

"Man, you know you're five times the loudmouth I am."

"Bullshit!"

The dinging bell announced the elevator's approach.

"Who else is up here that I know?"

"On this side, just me and Strunk. No, there's good snitching Rudy Wright."

"You mean hot head Rudy."

"That's him."

"How do you treat him?"

Rube put his finger to his lips and leaned forward. "The outside cut is right in front of his cell. His bars are cut, too."

"How'd that happen?"

"He moved into the cell. That's where Gilmore was. He just about had the bars cut when they took him downstairs."

"LOCK UP! LOCK UP!" a guard yelled from the front, banging his key for punctuation and emphasis.

"Hey, boss," Big Strunk yelled. "We only been out thirty-five minutes."

"Yeah, yeah, I know. I'll give you extra tomorrow."

Rube said, "That's old man Blair. He's ok."

"I don't think he's ever mistreated anybody in his life."

"See you *mañana*, brother," Jimmy Rube said, tapping the bars and heading toward his own cage.

Roger heard the gates slam and the bar drop. He thought of Rudy Wright. Rudy the heavyweight fighter – slow, clumsy and with a glass chin. Rudy the ignorant. Rudy the pervert who liked to suck dick and fuck young white boys. He muscled one kid, who stabbed him several times. Rudy was transferred to Folsom. He disliked Folsom. Its inhabitants tended toward grizzled old warriors who came out of their cells not caring if it rained dog shit or they died before lockup. Rudy wanted a transfer to a prison with younger convicts. To get a transfer, he testified for the prosecution in a prison murder. Despite Rudy's testimony, the jury acquitted the defendant. Still, Rudy got his transfer. Alas, the youths were unimpressed by a big black rat. Rudy killed one of them. The jury found him guilty and ordered him put to death. Here he was, two or three cells on the right. With his bars cut? Jesus, what strange alliances are made by circumstance. Roger's crime partner in the Death Row breakout was someone he found totally despicable.

Instead of unlocking more convicts to exercise, Sergeant Blair opened the gate for the Mail Room Officer. "Listen up," the man called. "If you want this certified mail, you goddamn sign for it. I'm not having the Post Office gimme any more shit about it because some idiot doesn't want to sign his name."

Roger wondered what was behind the declaration. He started to read a *New Yorker*'s Table of Contents, with part of his mind aware of voices near the front. The figure of the Mail Room Officer passed Roger's cell and stopped farther back. He then went the other way and disappeared.

After a minute or so, Rudy Wright called out, "Hey, Big Strunk."

"Yeah, Rudy?"

"What does 'judgement af . . . firmed' mean?"

"It means you go home tomorrow," called a previously unheard voice, eliciting a chorus of titters along the tier.

"Aw, man, quit jivin'," Rudy said. "It's bad news, ain't it?"

"Yeah, it's bad news," Big Strunk said.

Instead of absolute loathing for Rudy, who was everything despicable by convict values as well as those of society, Roger found some pity for the stupid brute. His absolute ignorance made him somehow less culpable. He was, like everyone, more or less what he had been taught by the teachers of life. What was that hoary bromide? "To understand all is to forgive all." That fell short of being a truth, but it came close enough to make him think. He could imagine Rudy's childhood. If God had a scale that weighed what most convicts had inflicted to what they had suffered, no doubt their own suffering would outweigh what they had meted out. Roger felt a strange new compassion for Rudy Wright.

Days turned into weeks. Cutting the outer bars was excruciatingly slow. Only during exercise could they work on it. The bridge game was cover. Seated cross-legged on the floor, Jellico rested his back against the outer bars and used the piece of hacksaw when the gun-walk guard was on the other side. Al Salas and Charlie Jackson were over there. The water had been forced out of their toilet by placing a pillow over its top, sitting on it and bouncing up and down. Roger did the same on this side because the bridge game was taking place directly in front of his cell. When the water was out of the toilets, they had a 'telephone' to the other side. The moment the gun-walk guard started to move, Salas or Jackson sounded the alarm through the toilet, and Roger relayed it to Jellico. When Jimmy Rube, Big Strunk, Robillard and Roger came out to exercise, they did calisthenics on the tier. To the guards watching from the front, it appeared quite natural. They relied on the gun-walk officer to patrol the tier. Rudy or Jellico kept his head in the toilet. The moment the gunman moved on the other side, he got the warning and relayed it with a loud cough. Even though they might saw for only a few seconds in a whole hour, it was hard for Roger to believe that nobody heard the hacksaw – and even harder to believe that nobody snitched.

Then it was done. The breakout would come the next stormy night, when rain would hide the sound of the hacksaw on the window.

The storm came four days later.

"Tonight," said Rube when they were out to shower.

"What about the hacksaw blade? It's getting dull."

"Oh, yeah. Why don't you run down to the hardware store for a new one?"

"We'll get it cut," Strunk said. "We'll have time, from midnight to eight in the morning. Nobody comes up here until they change shifts."

"By then it'll be broad daylight."

"Oh shit! That's right."

For the first time, Roger understood that Strunk was a little bit retarded. A man who planned escape for eighteen months and never thought of when the sun would rise had to be retarded.

"We've got five hours for sure," Jimmy Rube said. "I can chew through it in five hours."

"Okay, five hours. That's an awful dull blade and an awful thick bar."

"So whaddya wanna do? Give it up? Go back to our cells?"

"Hell, no!"

"Wait and give 'em a chance to find the cut bars?"

"Nope."

"So we throw the fuckin' dice and hope for seven."

"Don't use dice as an example," Strunk said. "I always throw snake eyes."

"Who's on duty tonight?"

"Sergeant Mencken and Deputy Dog."

"Is that right?" Although nobody knew for sure, it was believed that Sergeant Mencken was the executioner, he who took the extra pay to dip the gauze bag of cyanide pellets into the bucket of acid, creating cyanide gas. As for Deputy Dog, his nickname bespoke his nature.

"Do you think he'll make those check calls?"

"If he don't, he's in bad fuckin' trouble," Big Strunk said. "I don't like the motherfucker anyway. He's ready to kill me for a hundred and fifty dollars added to his paycheck."

"Is that all they pay him?"

"That's what I heard. They give him a day off, too."

"He'll make the check calls," Jimmy Rube said. "What would you do if you had a knife at your throat . . . and the guy holding it was under a death sentence already?"

Sergeant Blair banged a big key against the front bars. "Grab a hole! Lockup!"

Roger and his partners looked at each other and nodded. As Roger passed Rudy's cell, he grinned and winked and gave a slight thumbs-up signal. "Tonight," he said, embarrassed for his duplicity. Rudy was the lowest form of scum, a pervert child molester and a stoolpigeon. Yet Rudy was the fulcrum of escape; his cell bars were cut and he could crawl out. Indeed, there was no way to stop him short of calling the guard. He was big and strong and could be useful to Big Strunk in the takeover. Still, Roger tasted his own hypocrisy. It was a trait he particularly despised.

Roger entered his cell. The security bar came down and he heard the cell gates being locked. He was urinating with one hand on the wall when the key turned in his cell. "G'night Harper," said Sergeant Blair.

"G'night, Sarge," Roger said, adding "goodbye, too," in his mind.

Later, when Fast Eddie picked up the food trays, he commented, "Nobody's hungry. I hope it ain't the flu."

"Naw, just not hungry," Roger said, having barely touched the tray's contents.

The shift changed. The 4:00 pm to midnight crew came on. After the 4:30 count, the Sergeant passed out the mail. Roger got nothing. Richard Romero had eight letters. He had sharp, saturnine features and demonic good looks. Women wrote him from all over the world. Maybe I didn't kill enough people, Roger thought. The wryness of his thought was belied by the surge of anguish he felt when he remembered what he'd done.

"Hey, Roger," Rudy Wright called after the mail was passed out.

"Yeah, what's up?"

"They sent me an execution date," Rudy said. "June fifth. That's sixty-two days."

"We go together. I got one for the same day," came the seldom heard voice of Merkouris, who had killed his ex-wife, her new boyfriend and her nine-year-old son from a previous marriage. Afterward, he'd gone into a bar, ordered two drinks, "Bourbon for me. Scotch for my wife." He then pulled her head from a hatbox and put it on the plank. The bar emptied. The cops came. The jury turned thumbs down on an insanity defense and now, fourteen years later, the appeals were over and the trial court had issued a death warrant. He was a hundred pounds heavier than when he arrived. Roger remembered, for he had been in the county jail when the trial was in progress.

"It's gonna be crowded in there," Jimmy Rube said. "Rabbit Carson got a June 5th execution date."

"Who's Rabbit Carson?" someone asked.

"A dude over in the Adjustment Center," Strunk said: then, "Hey, Rudy, maybe they'll let you sit on Merkouris's lap."

Scattered laughter; silence from Rudy and Merkouris. Roger smiled. Sick shit, he thought, this bizarre talk of dates with death. Being on Death Row had a surreal aspect, a dream quality, something unbelievable. He'd imagined himself in prison, but not Death Row. It was part of the reason he'd chosen to heist drug dealers and pimps; nobody went to Death Row for killing scumbags. Nobody cared that they were dead – not that he had planned to kill anyone unless forced. As he leafed through the pages of events, he was unable to see where his decisions could have been different.

The flashing light told him the TV sets were turned on. He reached for the tiny earphones and the remote channel changer. It was his week to run things. He went through the channels and stopped on American Movie Classics. Brando and Karl Malden in "One Eyed Jacks". All right; maybe it would take his mind off things for a couple hours.

Ten o'clock. Another movie, Astaire dancing through London in "Royal Wedding." It made Roger ache to realize he would never see London, or anywhere else. Tonight's breakout was barely possible. The odds against them were immense. If they got out, imagine the manhunt for a bunch of condemned killers. He envisioned every Peace officer for hundreds of miles joining the hunt. It would take a miracle to get away. Shit, it would take a miracle to get out. In fact, it was already miraculous that they had cut their way through two sets of bars under the nose of the guards.

Then he wondered how many would go. How many could they let go? They had never talked about how many were going or who would be let out of their cells. It was too late to talk about now – until after things started to happen.

The movie was going off when the elevator bell rang out. The shift was changing. After that things would kick off.

The TV went off. A minute later the tier gate opened. The flashlight beams bounced from bars and across concrete floors. The new shift was coming down the tier, taking the count. As the footsteps got close, Roger shut his eyes and felt the light flash momentarily into his cell. When he heard them go out his armpits were slick with sweat. He could see rain running down the high windows.

The outer door opened and closed. The whir of the elevator marked its descent. Nobody would come up until morning. It had to start quickly. It was going to take hours to cut that fat window bar with half of a used hacksaw blade.

A black shadow showed on the outer bars. A moment later the gun-walk guard went by on rubber soles. He looked at the cells and the figures under blankets. Nobody sleeping, Roger thought, not up here. What about the French death penalty: you never knew when it would happen. Nobody told you. They came for you in the night. Damn, *nobody* at all sleeps there, thought Roger.

Down the tier he heard the hollow whump of someone jumping his rump on a pillow over the toilet, driving out the water to open the phone line to the other side.

Maybe I should do that to hear what's going on, Roger thought, and started to swing off the bunk. In the corner of his eye, a figure flashed by. Hey! It's happening. That was Big Strunk.

"What the fuck's happening', man!" called one of the two Crips.

"Shaddup, asshole!" Jimmy Rube snarled softy – but loud enough to hear. "Don't do no dry snitchin', punk!"

"Say, man –"

Another figure flew past Roger's cell, going the other way. It was Rudy Wright going to the Crip. Roger heard hissing words, then silence. His heart began to race. Pressing to the bars, off to the right he could see Big Strunk squeezing through his hole onto the gun-walk.

Rudy Wright returned, eyes white in his dark face. He had to wait, crouched down, behind Strunk, until the big man's feet disappeared through the bars. Rudy stretched out and wiggled through, disappearing around the corner.

Roger listened. One yell and Sergeant Mencken would be on the phone. Squeezing the cell bars, Roger visualized Stunk and Rudy waiting at the rear for Deputy Dog to come back along the cells, retracing his routine patrol.

A half cry, stifled. A splat of flesh on flesh. Roger closed his eyes and held his breath.

No shout of alarm.

A minute. Another. A figure appeared. It was Strunk. He wore the guard's hat, providing camouflage for his silhouette. He walked past Roger en route to the front. He'd taken the key to let him out. Rudy must be in the back with Deputy Dog. Roger could imagine Deputy Dog's terror at being helpless and at the whim of a condemned killer. He could also imagine that every inmate on Death Row #1 was standing at the bars, precisely as he was.

A voice, "... oh God!" The crash of a chair going over. A moment later, Big Strunk called out, "Rudy! Rudy! Bring him up here."

"Awright, awready?" Jimmy Rube called. "Hear it, Roger?"

"Does a bear shit in the woods?"

"Wha's goin' on, man?" asked one of the Crips.

As he spoke, the security bar went up. Big Strunk opened the outer gate and came onto the tier. Roger heard Jimmy Rube's cell gate being unlocked, then Robillard's. Strunk appeared. He had a Sergeant in tow. It was Sergeant Blair. The old man looked rumpled, his shirt askew, his hair mussed, a wild look in his eyes. As the key turned and Roger stepped out, he felt sorry for the old man – yet what could he do? Stop fighting for his life?

"Sorry, Sarge," Roger said. It issued without volition. It was politically incorrect in the hardcore code where kindness was weakness in the minds of most.

"Here you go," Strunk said, shoving Roger the .38 Police Special taken from the gun-walk guard. "You take the piece. You got the best sense. Watch. I'm gonna spring Salas and Charlie Jack."

Strunk hurried toward the front, passing Robillard and Rube. They were at a cell. Rube was waving his arms.

"Let's go, Sarge," Roger said, touching his shoulder without shoving. They moved toward the front. On the right, outside the bars and mesh, Rudy passed them. He was pushing Deputy Dog.

The guard's hands were behind his back, fastened with a belt. Rudy held onto that with one hand; in the other was the sharpened rod from the toilet bowl pushbutton. Its ice-pick point was aimed toward the guard's jugular.

Is this really happening, Roger thought as he passed Rube, who was talking heatedly to Richard Romero, his face shadowed so it exaggerated the angles of evil. His eyes glittered and he sneered his scorn. "I tell you, mon, you better, mon. Six six six . . . "

Roger kept moving, the Sergeant ahead of him, out into the light of the service area. Robillard was already there. A picnic-sized table was under the window. Even standing on that it would not be possible to reach up to the window. Robillard was putting a chair on the table. Whoever started cutting the bars would stand on that.

Roger heard noise from the tier. Rube rushed out, "Where's Strunk?"

"Gettin' Salas and Jackson."

"That fuckin' asshole, Romero, that sonofabitch – he says he's gonna start screamin' and breakin' up shit if we don't let him out of his cell. What about the rest?"

Sergeant Blair shook his head, as if the query was directed to him. "Not all those maniacs," he said.

"Wait'll Big Strunk gets back," Roger said. He opened the door to the office and motioned Sergeant Blair in. Rudy Wright arrived with Deputy Dog. Roger held the door until they passed in front of him. "Got a white man holdin' doors for me . . . damn!" Rudy Wright said. It was intended to be good natured and was taken as such. At the same time as Roger cracked a smile in return, he recollected that Rudy was a stoolpigeon and a rapist of young white boys and totally despicable even by the criminal codes of yesteryear. Rudy eyed the pistol hanging in Roger's hand, and rolled his eyes. Roger missed whatever it meant. He was taking Sergeant Blair's handcuffs from the belt holster.

"Siddown, 'dog motherfucker," Rudy said, pushing Deputy Dog down onto a desk chair with rollers.

"Uh uh," Roger said. "He can roll that around the room." Roger looked around. "Put him on his stomach and his hands around that table leg. Here –" he extended the handcuffs "– use these."

Rudy pulled the guard off the chair and shoved him down onto the floor. Roger moved the telephone away from the desk and told Sergeant Blair to sit on the floor behind the desk.

Salas and Jackson came in. Salas was an East LA *chicano* with enough muscles for a Greek statue – and enough tattoos to be the illustrated man. He and Jackson, a thief from another era, were on Death Row for a contract murder. A Santa Ana businessman wanted his partner iced, but he couldn't handle the guilt and went to the police. The businessman got Life; they got Death. Salas grinned and squeezed Roger's shoulder. "Hey, man, here we go –"

"Take it easy. We're a long way from out," Roger admonished. "Watch the Sergeant."

"Got him."

Rube and Strunk and Jellico. Where were they?

Right then, Jellico entered. The Death Row office was spartan – a desk, two chairs, a big table with a coffee maker and a refrigerator off to the side were its furnishings.

"Where're Rabe and Strunk?" Roger asked.

Jellico pointed toward the open tier gate. He went to the gate and looked down the tier. They were standing outside Romero's cell. He heard Romero's shrill demand, " . . . better lemme out!" The demand was followed by a loud rattle as he shook the bars.

To Roger's surprise, Rube reached out and unlocked the cell gate. Romero came out and all three came toward the gate. Behind Rube, someone called, and Rube said, "I'll be right back." A voice said, " . . . motherfucker better be back!"

Roger stepped aside as they came out. Big Strunk was first, winking as he went by. Next came Romero, tall and lean as an upright cobra. Rube was last, face serious. He didn't even look at Roger. Behind them were voices from the cells.

Robillard stood on the chair atop the table. He was starting to work on the window bars with the vintage hacksaw blade. The bars were half again the thickness of regular window bars.

"In there," Rube said, indicating the second door to the auxiliary room.

Romero's animal alarm sense rang bells. He balked, looked to Jimmy Rube and shook his head. "No. I wanna kill the guards."

Big Strunk hit him without warning. It was a right hand Sunday punch learned in California's gladiator schools. It would drop a heavyweight contender.

Richard Romero's jawbone fractured loudly, and he dropped shoulder first, onto the floor, his leg descending an instant afterward. He was OUT.

Strunk grimaced and held his right hand. Jimmy Rube dragged the inert form toward the door that Jellico now held open.

Suddenly, Romero began to thrash. "HELP! HELP! MURDER!" he screamed, his body coiling like something reptilian.

Roger started to run forward. Rube was there first, driving a foot into Romero's ribs, knocking out both wind and voice. Then Rube dropped on his body with both knees.

Summoned by the scream, Rudy Wright opened the office door. Roger grabbed the sharpened toilet bowl rod and fell upon the serial killer and devil worshipper. It would have taken the supernatural to save him. Roger stabbed once – below the ribs. The rod went in easily, and came out with suction. He stabbed again, hit rib bones and his hand slid down the rod. "Damn!"

Jimmy Rube pushed him aside. "Watch out." Rube had razor blades fused into toothbrush handles. He held Romero's hair in one hand and chopped at his throat with the other. Every time he chopped the flesh opened white then filled with blood. Romero was trying to fight and scream, but bare feet were kicking him so he could not breathe or yell aloud.

Finally, a chop in the wound and a geyser of thick arterial blood shot across the room onto the wall, as if sprayed from a hose. The struggles receded to spasms, and then he was still.

Robillard went back to work. "C'mon," Rube said to Roger, grabbing one of Romero's feet.

They dragged the corpse back onto the tier, leaving a wide swathe of blood across the waxed concrete floor. When they dropped him, Rube stood over him. "Anybody else wanna come out before we tell 'em?"

"Naw, man, you runnin' shit around here," said a voice – and all concurred by the subsequent silence.

Just then, Roger remembered and said, "The check call."

"Yeah. Oh shit!"

They hurried off the tier. Jellico had relieved Robillard atop the chair. The office door was open. Jackson and Strunk were close around Sergeant Blair. They had the telephone on the desk in front of him. His hands were tied. Jackson picked up the telephone receiver and dialed Operator. The check call was with the prison switchboard. Everyone held their breath and listened closely. "Operator," said the Switchboard Operator.

Roger held the receiver up to Sergeant Blair. "Blair and Powell on the row," he said.

"Okay." The operator hung up.

Strunk replaced the receiver. "That's good, Sarge."

Roger saw that the old man had tears in his eyes, and Roger suddenly wanted to cry, too. It was a terrible thing to do to a nice old man, but he was fighting for his life.

Roger went out of the office. Jellico was still at the window. The door to the other room was open. Salas was working on the double-door metal cabinet that contained various barbiturates and tranquilizers and, maybe, some painkillers. Rumor said the man being executed was given his choice of a double of bourbon or a shot of morphine before they took him into the gas chamber. Maybe it was true, maybe it wasn't. The only two guys to be taken down to the overnight condemned cells in twenty-five years had failed to return and tell what happened. Whatever the truth, Salas had found a screwdriver in a drawer and was starting to work on the cabinet. He rammed it into a crack and worked it around. It was going to take time, but eventually he would pop the door open. Whether he got out or not, he was going to get loaded. In fact, that was all he wanted if he got away.

Strunk went by and climbed onto the table. Jellico stepped off the chair and handed Strunk the hacksaw. Big Strunk went to work, pressing down on the worn hacksaw blade, his muscled shoulders gleaming with sweat. Tension as much as exertion, Roger thought, going over to see the progress.

The hacksaw had cut into the bar. It was farther along than Roger expected, but there was still a lot to cut. The bar had to be cut twice; it was too thick to bend. Big Strunk looked down and grinned. "It's movin', bro."

"Don't stop to talk, fool. Get to work," Roger said. Strunk turned and began cutting with the hacksaw. Roger looked around and wondered whether what he saw was truth or delusion. Here he was on Death Row with the worst murderers, those sentenced to die, running loose. Thank God he had the pistol. He'd tried to put it in his waistband, but without a belt it wouldn't work. He carried it in his hand. It was faster that way – if he needed it.

Where was Jackson? Roger went to look through the open office door. Rudy Wright was seated above Deputy Dog, who was still on his belly with his manacled hands fastened around the table leg.

Sergeant Blair slumped in the corner, a torn bed sheet wrapped around his torso, holding his arms next to his body. Robillard was watching over him. "Roger," said Robillard. "You watch him. I gotta take a piss."

"Go on," said Roger, then sat on the edge of the desk. The Sergeant's eyes had a vacant glaze and his face was blotchy and pale. "You okay, Sarge?" he asked, aware of the man's age and the many Camels he smoked. Sergeant Blair gave the slightest nod.

Jimmy Rube and Charlie Jackson came into the office. Rube was excited. "Man, we're gonna get outta this motherfucker. Go check it out, Roger. I'll watch him. It's time for the check call anyway."

Rube moved the phone to the desk. Roger went out and looked. It was true. Big Strunk was halfway through the bar. It had taken a little over half an hour. By 3:30 they could climb through the window just above the outside gun-rail and just below the administration building roof. What then? They couldn't all crawl out together. He'd have to talk to Rube and Strunk about it. What if someone disrupted them? "I've got the pistol," Roger muttered. Of course, it would be all over the moment he fired a shot. He might as well put the last one in his own mouth.

Suddenly, there was a loud crash. Goddamn! Roger hurried to the auxiliary room. Salas had popped the cabinet door. That was the noise. The powerful Mexican was rifling through the contents of the medicine locker, throwing what he didn't want into a wastebasket.

Roger looked to the sky for patience. Salas turned. "I'm sorry, man. I got . . . frustrated, y'know what I mean?"

"Try to be quiet, man. Please. They can hear that shit downstairs."

"Yeah . . . yeah," said Salas, showing his total resentment at being told anything by anyone.

As Roger turned away, Jimmy Rube came out of the office. "You seen Jellico?"

"Not for a few minutes."

"Find the motherfucker. Big Strunk needs some relief."

"We gotta talk, too. We don't know how the fuck we're gonna do this."

"Whaddya mean?"

"That gun tower is gonna spot us, man, if all of us crawl out together. And what about all those guys locked up? We gonna leave 'em locked up? They're gonna go crazy when they realize we're gone and they're still locked up."

"Get Jellico. Then us three can cut it up."

Roger nodded and turned. Two rooms, two tiers and the area where they stood; Jellico had to be close. He looked into the auxiliary room. Salas and Jackson were at the big sink used for cleaning mops. Salas threw a handful of pills into his mouth and leaned over to get the water. "Where's Jellico?" asked Roger.

"On the tier, I think," said Jackson. "Probably visitin' that little fruiter Cocoa." Salas stepped away from the sink and Jackson stepped up to the faucet with a mouthful of pills.

At the gate, Roger looked down the tier. It was black shadows and distant light. Shapes were visible but not colors. He didn't see anyone on the tier. Roger went to the other side. It was better lighted because it faced the Big Yard, and the yard's floodlights reached through the high windows. Jellico must be on the other side, after all.

"Hey, man! Hey! On the tier!"

It was one of the Crips. For a moment Roger considered ignoring the call. Then he started down the tier. "Yeah, what's up?" he asked. He was barefoot and suddenly he was sticking to the concrete floor. "What the . . . " he stepped aside and looked down. He'd walked into the trail of blood that Romero had leaked when he was dragged across the floor.

It was thick and sticky between Roger's toes. "Shit!"

He headed toward his own open cell gate, for a wet towel to wipe it off. As he passed the Crips he said, "I'll be back."

"Damn, a nigger'll get dissed on Death Row real quick," one said. For some reason it made Roger burst into laughter. Then he remembered he was looking through the bars at faces of caged killers, their eyes glittering. Several called out to him, "Hey, man, hey, hey . . . " He kept going.

Suddenly a figure jumped back from outside the bars. He'd been hidden because the walls between cells extended outward.

Roger was startled. Then he recognized Jellico – and at the same moment glanced toward the cell bars, where he saw a black transvestite called Cocoa, who was standing on the bunk next to the bars. When Roger looked, Cocoa was stuffing his erection back in his jeans. Jellico had been sucking a dick. Damn! What a phantasmagorical world this was.

Roger took it in in one second, and reacted. Then he thought, none of my business. He said to Jellico, "Hey, they want you to take over from Big Strunk."

Roger started to move on. Jellico stepped in front of him. His face was contorted. 'If you say a word, man, I'll kill you like–"

Roger turned his body so Jellico couldn't grab the pistol. "What're you talking about?" Roger said. "Whaddya mean, 'say a word . . . '?"

Jellico stopped, looked puzzled. "Never mind."

"Go take over," Roger said. "You want out, don't you?"

Jellico hurried off. Roger watched the hulking figure, and he was suddenly certain that Jellico had killed the four gay men in San Francisco after having sex. Jellico had killed to keep them quiet. Roger had seen the same thing once in Folsom. Early in the morning he heard the screams – they all heard the screams – and, on the tier below, a young boy was stabbed to death by his cell partner. The boy had told him about the cell partner, who had a reputation as one of Folsom's deadliest killers. What Roger had just witnessed reeked of sameness, especially with Jellico's tirade. Who cares, Roger thought? Jellico cares, that's who. Somebody sure twisted his head once upon a time.

In the cell, Roger grabbed a t-shirt and put his foot in the toilet, rubbing the sticky blood away with his fingers. He wiped his foot with the t-shirt; then put his other foot in the toilet bowl and repeated the process. He'd better get something on his feet if he was going to climb over the roof, drop to the ground and run through the countryside. He put on two layers of socks. He would try to find something more – but nobody had shoes up here, or did they?

He made his way to the front. Jellico was working on the window bars. Rube and Strunk awaited him.

"We gotta decide how we're gonna do this."

"Whaddya mean?" Strunk asked.

"We can't all go out that window together," Roger said. "It'd be like a herd of buffalo goin' across the roof."

"We'll go two at a time," said Rube. "Me and Strunk; then you and Robillard."

"That sounds great . . . but what're these fools gonna do when we're gone?"

As if intended as an example of what to expect, Salas came out of the auxiliary room. His face was twisted in torment. "I'm gonna go puke and lie down." He staggered past them and disappeared onto the tier.

"See what I mean?" Roger said.

"What happened to him?"

"He got in that medicine locker."

"Awww, shit! They're so dumb you wonder how they found the place to commit the crime."

"Personally," said Strunk, "I don't give a rat's ass what they do when I'm gone."

"As long as they wait until we're over the wall," Rube added.

Roger worried what Rudy Wright, or even some of those in the cells, might do to Sergeant Blair, but voicing such concerns would be viewed askance, if not derided. Instead he asked, "Which way you goin' when you get outta the wall?"

"Probably up the road toward the old rock quarry," Rube answered. "Circle around that hill and across those flats toward Corte Madera. We'll wait fifteen minutes at the quarry."

Roger was certain they would want the pistol, but apparently they'd forgotten all about it, for they said nothing and he followed suit.

"Let's go see how he's doin'," Rube said, indicating Jellico at the window.

"It's about time for another check call," Strunk said.

"Right."

When they approached the table, they saw the hacksaw sever the window bar. "Lemme up there," Strunk said. "See if I can bend that motherfucker."

Jellico stepped down and Strunk stepped up. He grabbed the bar and stepped onto the window ledge, bending at the waist and coiling his body so he had all his massive strength, including his legs, focused. He strained, his muscles stood out. "Nothing," he said. "Gimme the hacksaw."

Jellico handed it over and jumped off the table. Roger gave his arm a comradely shake. "Good work," he said. Jellico nodded without looking at him. Big Strunk started the second cut in the window bar. Without the storm to hide the sound, the hacksaw would have been heard throughout the San Quentin night.

"C'mon, let's tell 'em the rules," Rube said, heading toward the office. "Here's how we're doin' it," he said to Rudy and Robillard. As Rube told them the plan, Roger thought of something else. Alarms would sound the moment the check call was overdue. To have any chance at getting away – barefoot in the rain – required half a mile headstart. Even then, it would be a long shot. Anything less and they might as well surrender. The last people to leave had to go immediately after a check call to have any kind of headstart – and they had to make sure Sergeant Blair and Deputy Dog didn't sound the alarm. Locking them in a cell was the best way. Romero's was empty. Then Roger realized they could also kill the old man and Deputy Dog. They could do whatever they wanted to Deputy Dog, but Sergeant Blair had never knowingly harmed anyone in the decade Roger had known him, and probably not before that. He was determined that nothing was going to happen to Sergeant Blair. I should be able to cover that bet, he thought, but he felt the added stress of that decision. It changed how he would play things, although the specifics were still vague.

Roger wondered how Salas was doing and started down the tier. Again the face; the voices, "Hey, man! Hey, Roger . . . "

"Take it easy," he said. "It's gonna be all right. If we get somethin' down, all you crazy motherfuckers can run wild across the Bay Area." What a dirty lie he was telling them. What else could he do? The truth would drive them crazy. It would be a cold day in Palm Springs before he sprung this crew of madmen. Most of them he would execute himself. Then he saw McGurk's face. Poor McGurk. Busted for drunk driving in Fresno, they put him in a cell with a rapist who'd nailed a chick he knew. McGurk socked the pervert, the guy's head hit the edge of the bed. He came from a rich white family, and McGurk wound up being sentenced to die for what should have been manslaughter. There was a time when McGurk would have gotten an appeals court reversal. Now it was shaky.

Roger looked into Salas' cell. The Mexican was on his side, out like a light, curled up with his hands between his knees. It was somehow obscene that he would leave himself so vulnerable on Death Row, with wall-to-wall killers running wild.

No use waking him up. They'll probably bust him right where he is. He didn't want to escape. He just wanted to get high.

As Roger walked out, the hacksaw's rasp stopped. Was something wrong?

When he stepped off the dark tier into the lighted front section, Rube, Jackson and Jellico were watching Big Strunk, who had the bar in both hands, both feet planted on the wall, so he was bent in half and jutting out. His muscles suddenly stood out as he put all his strength into it. He'd cut partway through. Was it enough to make it move? If so, they could worry it back and forth and it would snap – just like a big paper clip.

"Yeah!" Big Strunk said in a guttural gasp, stepping down and looking around. "It moved. The motherfucker moved . . . !"

"Move over," said Rube. "Lemme help."

Together they grabbed the bar and tried to work it back and forth. "Cut some more," Rube said. "Just a little bit."

Strunk went to work with a frenzy. A few more minutes and they would be on the roof in the rain.

Roger went to the office. Sergeant Blair was making the check call to the prison switchboard, "Death Row check call . . . Blair and Powell."

"What's goin' on out there?" Rudy Wright asked.

"Any minute now."

Rudy had his bare foot on Deputy Dog's back. He raised his heel and brought it down hard. "You hear that, boy?"

Officer Powell gasped in pain. His face was turned toward Roger and his terror was evident. Roger felt no compassion for him. The nickname Deputy Dog came from how he treated convicts, and he was especially contemptuous if they were black.

The snap of the window bar was a small explosion. Roger turned to the door. Rube appeared. He grinned and circled thumb and forefinger in the sign of OK, and turned away.

Roger went to the office door and looked. Big Strunk was already squeezing through headfirst. He disappeared into the wet night, and Rube was right behind him.

"Yeah, pig," Rudy Wright said. "They're gone and pretty soon it's gonna be you and me."

"How you doin', Sarge?" Roger asked.

Sergeant Blair shook his head.

Jellico appeared. "Hey, that guy's goin' out the window."

"What?"

"Jackson's goin' now."

Roger rushed out. Jackson was sliding out the window feet first. Roger saw his head and shoulders disappear. Jackson waved and grinned like the Cheshire Cat.

A cry of pain turned Roger back into the office. Rudy Wright was bending over Deputy Dog. His thick dark fingers were entwined in the guard's hair; he was pulling up the head and ramming it back into the floor. "How's that, punk ass pig?"

"Jesus Christ," cried Sergeant Blair. "Make him stop."

Roger was already keyed up from watching Jackson's premature escape. He needed the Sergeant. "Freeze on that shit," he said to Rudy Wright.

The black man uncoiled, holding Deputy Dog's hair in one hand and the long toilet rod with ice-pick point in the other. "What say, white boy? Who the fuck you think you are?"

"Nigger, I'm the peckerwood that'll blow your head off," he raised his arm, simultaneously thumbing back the hammer on the .38 Smith and Wesson service revolver. "Get outta here. Go on!" His face left no doubt of his determination.

Rudy Wright hesitated. He was one stride and a dive away. He was big, fast and strong. The turning gears of his brain were evident.

"Go on . . . make history," Roger said. "I wanna kill ya."

The amber eyes in the dark face were an inferno of scorn and hatred – but he turned away. "White trash motherfucker," he said as he went out the door.

Roger started to laugh at the words. At some point, insults are meaningless.

"Oh man," said Robillard. "I thought it was gonna go down. I'll close the door."

"No. I gotta watch the window. I don't want another one climbing out ahead of time."

"It's time for you and me."

Roger looked at Sergeant Blair – and the old man looked terrible. "You go first," he said.

"Somebody's gotta watch these two," Robillard said.

"You wanna go or not?"

"Hell, yes. I wanna die fightin', or runnin' . . . or somethin'."

"I'll watch them from the door. I'll be right behind you."

A scream of pain and terror filled Death Row.

Roger ran to the office door. The screams continued. They were down a tier.

"Watch 'em," Roger said, then started toward the cries. What the hell was going on?

When he reached the front end of the tier, he saw a cluster of figures stepping back from a falling body. It took a moment to realize what had happened: Rudy Wright had taken the key and opened cells. In the dim light only the figures were visible. They started toward the front.

"Hold it right there!" Roger yelled, raising the pistol.

The group fragmented into figures. Some ducked next to the cells, behind the protruding cell walls. Others pressed against the bars. They kept coming.

"Outta the way," someone yelled.

"You better stop," he called. The figures next to the cells were jumping forward one cell wall at a time. Those against the outer bars were hard to see. Were they inching forward?

"Shoot, sucker. We're dyin' anyway." Other voices: "Rush the motherfucker." "Fuck that honky." Another said, "Give it up, man."

The racial cry reminded Roger that two were called the Zebra Killers. For months they had cruised the Bay Area, killing whites simply because they were white. If not for this fact his natural alliance with the outlaw would have dominated.

A figure came from a jutting cell wall.

Roger fired. The pistol jumped, the sound awesome as it bounced from the concrete cell-house walls. The figure's leg went out from under him.

An instant of silence. Then they started working themselves up to charge. Roger went back to the office door. He could cover the gate onto the tier. A head peeked out, then pulled back.

The telephone rang – and kept ringing.

Suddenly the night outside was turned to day as gigantic floodlights were turned on. The cell-block windows brightened.

'It's all over, isn't it?" Robillard said.

Roger nodded without taking his eyes from the gate.

"I'm going to tell them you saved our lives," Sergeant Blair said.

Roger managed a half smile. "That might not be a favor, Sarge."

"Should I answer the phone?"

"Yeah. Go ahead. Tell 'em to get up here quick."

Sergeant Blair picked up the phone.

From the distance came the sound of gunfire. Roger closed his eyes. He'd hoped that his friends had gotten away. That seemed unlikely now.

Roger kept his eye on the tier gate. When he heard the ding ding of the elevator's arrival, and the sound of the key on the outer door, he knew it was the end. He put the revolver to his temple and squeezed the trigger.

THE LIFE AHEAD

It was early Friday afternoon and, as usual, the poker game had been going on since the gates opened following the morning cleanup. On Monday the men with money in their accounts could draw out $20. For a day or two there were more gamblers than there were seats. By now, however, the game was down to the usual four, plus one newcomer. Max Black was one of the four. Just nineteen, he was a good poker player. He'd been playing with grown men since he was fifteen. He'd lied about his age so he would be put in an adult tank. Juveniles stayed locked in their cells twenty-four hours a day. This was better. Indeed, he managed to support himself in the jailhouse economy by playing poker. He'd been in this tank for eleven months awaiting trial and disposition, and he played poker every day, all day and evening, too, except when he went to court. He had honed his skill against tough poker players.

Today, however, he was losing. He'd lost in court, too, but was expecting that. He was getting mediocre hands, not really bad hands, which wouldn't have been a disaster, for he would have simply thrown bad hands away. He was getting second best hands and was playing them poorly, pushing too hard when caution was the right move. He was also distracted. Half his hearing and his eyes were tuned for the call to "Roll 'em Up." The northbound prison bus departed sometime between 5:00 and 7:00 this afternoon. Every time he heard keys jangle nearby, he anticipated being called to roll up.

Indeed, just as Six Way Jack made a big bet, he imagined hearing the call in another tank. "Fire away," he muttered and reached for his chips and started counting them into the pot. Even before he finished, he knew he had a loser. Six Way Jack never bluffed, and Max's own hand was okay, a small straight, but not with Jack and Jack's bet.

"All blue," Jack said. He had a flush, all spades, from the Ace, Queen.

Max threw his cards in the air. "Shit . . . "

"Hey . . . hey," said Tex Silcox. "Easy on the cards, man."

Max nodded. "Okay . . . Anyway, I quit."

As he was cashing in his chips, from the front of the tank, eight cells away, came the sound of a heavy steel key banging the gate. "Black! Cell six . . . Roll 'em up for the gray goose." That was the name given to the corrections bus.

Max had already bundled his gear and left it on the foot of his bunk. He went to his cell and took his bankroll of six $20 bills from his pocket. They were rolled tight and wrapped in polyurethane. He had forty dollars in $1 and $5 bills that he had been using in the poker game. His cell partner, Bill Savage, was on the top bunk. He had put down a paperback book when Max appeared. "You're outta here, huh?" he asked.

"Yeah, I'm gone," Max said. "Here. Take this." He handed Savage the poker game money.

"What's this for?"

"'Cause I can't take it with me. It's too much to put up my ass."

"Okay. Thanks, bro'."

Using Vaseline from a tube, Max greased the polyurethane wrapped twenties and, grimacing, worked them into his rectum. "I'll probably give myself hemorrhoids or something." Cash money was contraband in prison, but worth twice as much as money on the books.

Bang! Bang! Bang! The key sounded on the gate. "Okay, Black! Roll out!"

"Comin', boss," Max called back. When he came out of the cell, half a dozen jailhouse friends were waiting to say goodbye, wishing him luck, and slapping him on the back. Ebie, the older of two brothers from North Hollywood, was there. "Hey, Max, be cool. I'll see you in a week or two." Ebie had been sentenced yesterday. Max had known him since juvenile hall when they were twelve. He was a friend and respected. He was a homely dog, with a flat face, bad teeth and bow legs. He was borderline illiterate, but he was street-smart and had a colorful phrasing in his conversation, even if he couldn't read a matchbook cover.

The space at the gate was narrow, so some goodbyes were said over shoulders as Max waited for the deputy to key the gate. "See you guys later," he said as the deputy pulled it open and stepped back. "You know where to go, Black."

"Follow the yellow brick road."

The deputy nodded. On the jail floor were colored stripes side-by-side. The yellow one led to the shower room where releases got their clothes. Those going free changed there. Those going in custody went down to a narrow stair to a bullpen. The red stripe went to the visiting room, the green to the Attorney Room, the black to the infirmary.

At the show room, Max showed his property slip to the trusty, who checked him off a list and got his clothes.

The bullpen had about twenty prisoners. More would appear. The "gray goose" rarely made its run with an empty seat. There were prison guards who would escort them, already at work chaining each man up in leg-irons and wrist-irons and then chaining each man to the next. This was no jail he was going to. This was the big show.

Max was getting excited. He was nineteen years old, and was the youngest guy in the group. He had spent half of his life in juvenile detention or in local jails. He had half a dozen convictions on his growing rap sheet, but now he was going up on a felony that carried a seven-year rap. He'd still be young when he got out. It was like going to school. He'd come out of the joint smarter, wiser. They wouldn't get him a second time. But so what, if they did.

The adrenaline rush in pulling off a successful robbery was better than sex. Better than drugs. Better than anything else he'd ever experienced.

Don't do the crime, if you are not prepared to do the time, he was told. Max was prepared to do both.

EBOOKS BY EDWARD BUNKER

FROM MYSTERIOUSPRESS.COM
AND OPEN ROAD MEDIA

Available wherever ebooks are sold

MYSTERIOUSPRESS.COM

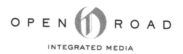

OPEN ROAD
INTEGRATED MEDIA

MYSTERIOUSPRESS.COM

Otto Penzler, owner of the Mysterious Bookshop in Manhattan, founded the Mysterious Press in 1975. Penzler quickly became known for his outstanding selection of mystery, crime, and suspense books, both from his imprint and in his store. The imprint was devoted to printing the best books in these genres, using fine paper and top dust-jacket artists, as well as offering many limited, signed editions.

Now the Mysterious Press has gone digital, publishing ebooks through **MysteriousPress.com**.

MysteriousPress.com offers readers essential noir and suspense fiction, hard-boiled crime novels, and the latest thrillers from both debut authors and mystery masters. Discover classics and new voices, all from one legendary source.

FIND OUT MORE AT

WWW.MYSTERIOUSPRESS.COM

FOLLOW US:

@emysteries and Facebook.com/MysteriousPressCom

MysteriousPress.com is one of a select group of publishing partners of Open Road Integrated Media, Inc.

OPEN ROAD
INTEGRATED MEDIA

Open Road Integrated Media is a digital publisher and multimedia content company. Open Road creates connections between authors and their audiences by marketing its ebooks through a new proprietary online platform, which uses premium video content and social media.

Videos, Archival Documents, and New Releases

Sign up for the Open Road Media newsletter and get news delivered straight to your inbox.

Sign up now at
www.openroadmedia.com/newsletters

FIND OUT MORE AT
WWW.OPENROADMEDIA.COM

FOLLOW US:
@openroadmedia and
Facebook.com/OpenRoadMedia

CPSIA information can be obtained
at www.ICGtesting.com
Printed in the USA
JSHW021923170521
14857JS00001B/59